THE HOME FOR
WAYWARD PARROTS

THE HOME

FOR
WAYWARD

PARROTS

DARUSHA WEHM

NEWEST PRESS
EDMONTON, AB

Library and Archives Canada Cataloguing in Publication

Wehm, M. Darusha, 1975-, author
The home for wayward parrots / Darusha Wehm.

Issued in print and electronic formats.
ISBN 978-1-988732-27-5 (softcover).--ISBN 978-1-988732-28-2 (EPUB).--
ISBN 978-1-988732-29-9 (Kindle)

I. Title.

PS8645.E347H66 2018   C813'.6   C2017-905220-9
                                               C2017-905221-7

Board Editor: Leslie Vermeer
Cover design & layout: Kate Hargreaves
Author photograph: Steven Ensslen
Cover photograph: Andrew Pons (Creative Commons via Unsplash,
image has been modified)

NeWest Press acknowledges the support of the Canada Council for the Arts, the Alberta Foundation for the Arts, and the Edmonton Arts Council for support of our publishing program. This project is funded in part by the Government of Canada.

201, 8540 – 109 Street
Edmonton, AB T6G 1E6
780.432.9427
NeWest Press   www.newestpress.com

No bison were harmed in the making of this book.
PRINTED AND BOUND IN CANADA
1 2 3 4 5 20 19 18

For Clara Katherine

CONTENTS

1
GUMBO

I **WAS SITTING ON THE TOILET** the first time I ever spoke with
my mother. It was a bad habit, taking the phone into the
bathroom, but I did it every time. Ever since I got one of
those phones with the internet and everything, I'd find myself
surfing while taking a crap. I figure that it's just the twenty-
first–century equivalent of reading the sports section on the
john. Of course, the sports section never rings with the phone
call you've been wanting to get for thirty years.

Don't get me wrong — I grew up with a mom and dad
just like about half the rest of the world. It was almost like the
descriptions in a badly written children's book; we lived in a
white clapboard house on a tree-lined street in a quaint little
town. The reality is that I don't even know what clapboard is,
and the house was blue, except for the year my dad got creative.
Mom repainted it the next summer. Blue.

I think she liked the blue because Mom was a cop. When I
was little I thought her first name was Officer. I think she would
have worn her uniform on her days off if she were allowed. On
the other hand, unless you lived with us, you'd hardly even know
that Dad had a job. Some people thought he was embarrassed —
he was a nurse — but really it was that he didn't care about work
like Mom did. Dad was a good nurse, but he didn't love nursing
like Mom loved policing. It was just a job for him and he left the
patients at the hospital. Being a cop was like Mom's religion.

Other kids used to make fun of me because of Mom and Dad. "Does your dad wear an apron, too?" they'd ask. I knew it was supposed to be mean, but he did wear an apron sometimes. It never seemed weird to me, because it's just what was normal in my house. Looking back, I guess I'm lucky they named me Brian; I could have been saddled with one of those horrible gender-neutral monikers you see everywhere these days. Logan, Mason and Taylor, like some kind of unisex law firm.

I was lucky in a lot of ways, I know. My parents never let me forget that they loved me; they even spun the whole adopted thing as a way of proving it. They *picked* me — I was no accident. And I love my folks just fine, but I can't say I never thought about it. To be honest, I thought about the fact that I was adopted all the time.

I GUESS NOWADAYS YOU'D SAY we lived in the suburbs, but everyone just called it out of town. It was a half-hour car ride into downtown, but it was nothing like living in the city. Even now, Saanich isn't like what I imagine when I think of the 'burbs. We had a quarter acre of our own and the down-the-road neighbours had a small dairy farm. The neighbourhood smelled like trees and horses.

Growing up in Saanich was kind of weird. It wasn't the country — I mean it was less than an hour on the bus to anywhere in Victoria, and the bus ran every day. Once I got older it seemed I spent more hours on the bus than anywhere else. That bus was like a second home until I moved into the city after university.

But we lived a lot like country people do, I imagine. The neighbourhood kids all ran around feral in the summers. When my folks would kick me out of the house to "get some fresh air instead of spending all your time with your nose in a book," I'd spend the entire day in the woods with Johnny Frazier, Blair McKirk and Angela Hoeffer. We'd leave our houses first thing in the morning and tear around on our bikes until six or seven at night.

I can't remember us ever doing anything particularly interesting, but we somehow managed to entertain ourselves in those days. I guess it's not really that hard to amuse a bunch of ten-year-olds. The big excitement one summer was this abandoned construction project on the other side of the highway. Crossing the highway was a big deal because we weren't supposed to do it. There weren't really that many rules, but of course we had to break the ones there were. So crossing the highway without getting caught was the major goal of almost every excursion. And once we found the lot, we were in kid heaven.

I don't know what we found so exciting about the place. I guess the construction people cleared away anything of value before they took off. There were no dead bodies, buried treasure or working heavy machinery to be found. But at the time we all thought it was the best place ever. Angela found it first, and she never stopped reminding us it was thanks to her that we had the coolest hangout around.

I was sitting on The Mound, this hill of dirt we claimed as the main meeting spot. It was my turn to bring the food, and I had a bunch of peanut butter and honey sandwiches in my backpack. I handed one to Johnny, who started wolfing it down before I'd even managed to give out the rest of them. Typical.

"Jesus, Johnny," Blair said, taking the wax-paper package from me and rolling his eyes. "Your mom doesn't feed you or what?"

"Shut up," Johnny said around a mouthful of sandwich. This was a daily exchange between the two and neither I nor Angela even heard it anymore. I passed her a sandwich and unwrapped my own. The four of us chewed for a while without talking. Blair pulled out a two-litre bottle of Coke wrapped in a paper bag and we passed it around like it was rotgut wine and we were a pack of hobos. We were all envious of Blair. His parents were getting divorced, and as a result he and his two sisters could get anything they wanted. This largesse trickled down to our gang in the form of Coke, bags of Old Dutch potato chips and the occasional candy bar.

"We should go look for tools behind the shed," Angela said after half her sandwich was gone.

"There's nothing here," I argued. We'd looked for something decent every day for a week and never found anything left behind.

"We haven't looked everywhere," Blair said, looking toward Angela. Everyone knew he liked her, except her and maybe him.

"You got any other ideas, Gumbo?" she asked me as if Blair hadn't said a word. If it bothered him, he didn't show it.

I was the only one in our group with a nickname, and I was never sure whether I liked the unique status or not. It was one of those dumb things that doesn't make any sense but sticks with you forever. When we were all little, we would go out trick-or-treating on Halloween together. One year — I was maybe seven — I dressed as an elephant. I don't know where I got the idea or how Dad even pulled it off. He was responsible for stuff like that, though if I'd wanted to be a cop for Halloween I'm sure Mom would have dug up a genuine child-sized uniform for me. I was never once a cop for Halloween.

Anyway, I was dressed up in grey sweats stuffed with pillows and an elephant mask with giant floppy ears and a trunk that hung to my knees. It looked ridiculous, but at least it was warm. The others were already there when Mom dropped me off at Johnny's house. She walked me up to the door and delivered me to Mrs. Frazier with her annual Halloween warning about flashlights, reflective clothing and razor blades, and I had the usual sensation of wanting the floor to swallow me up. Having a cop for a mom is a permanent state of embarrassment.

After my blush faded, Johnny's little sister Mary came toddling out to the door. She took one look at me and started jumping up and down and giggling. "Gumbo," she shouted in that little-kid voice. "Gumbo, Gumbo, Gumbo!"

At first we though she was trying to say my last name, but how would she even know what it was? She was only three. After a second or two of confusion, we all figured out that she was trying to say Dumbo. It was her current favourite movie, and the Fraziers had even bought the VHS tape for their new VCR. I guess I should be glad that she couldn't pronounce it right. I don't know if I could stand to be known as Brian Dumbo.

"You got any chips, Blair?" I asked, deflecting Angela's question. I didn't have any ideas, but I was getting tired of digging in the dirt for non-existent treasures. They been going out to the site every day for a couple of weeks, and Mom and Dad had sent me out with them more days than they hadn't. The novelty was starting to wear off.

Angela wasn't easily ignored, though. She intercepted the bag of Rip-L chips that Blair tossed me and said, "Hang on, Gum. You got something you want to do this afternoon? Digging for tools isn't good enough for you? You got some hot book you wanna read? Or do you need to go dust for prints somewhere?" My face got hot, and I wished I'd never mentioned the Junior Detective Kit I'd gotten for my birthday that year.

"Come on, Angela," Johnny said, hand wrist deep in his own bag of chips. "Don't be a jerk."

"Never mind," I said, getting up and wiping the dirt from my butt. "I just don't feel like it today." I half walked, half fell down The Mound toward where the bikes were lying on the ground.

"Where are you going?" Blair called after me.

"Home," I said, not turning around. I picked up my bike and walked it over to the edge of the lot.

As I looked for my opening to cross the highway, I heard Angela laugh a fake high-pitched titter. I knew then that she felt bad, but it was too late. I was already halfway across the highway and heading for home.

IT WAS SOMETIME IN THE SUMMER of the construction lot that I first discovered it might be possible to find out who my real parents were. I never called them that out loud; I knew that Mom and Dad would die if they heard me say that. But that's what they were in my mind. My real parents. And I could maybe find them someday. The thought of it consumed me the summer I was ten years old.

And it consumed me every summer, every winter, every spring and fall for twenty more years, until the one morning I was in the john reading comics on my phone and it rang.

2
STAYING OVER FOR DINNER

I N A LOT OF WAYS, the four of us shared one combined childhood. I would probably have been perfectly happy just to sit
in my room, reading my books or making an inventory of
my toys, but Mom and Dad made sure I got "out with people."
And people meant Johnny, Blair and Ange. We were in and out
of each other's houses without prejudice in some combination
or another. I think there were probably times when a group of
us would find ourselves in some house and we'd realize that the
kid whose house it was wasn't even there. It was this closeness
that made what happened with Jacquie even more awful.

For all the time we spent at each other's places, I hated
going over to someone's house for dinner. I wasn't exactly a
picky eater — I'd try anything and there wasn't much I really
didn't like — but it drove me crazy to have food served in the
wrong order. It has always been obvious to me that there is a
clear order in which dishes should be put on plates, but no one
else seems to understand it. As I got older I was mostly able to
just let it go, but when I was a kid it made eating at someone
else's house an almost physically painful process.

And then there was everything else that was horrible and
awkward about being part of that incredibly intimate family
ritual of dinnertime. All the other kids' houses were weird
and I never knew how to act. I dreaded going over for dinner.
Especially at the McKirks'.

For the longest time, we all tried to stay out of the McKirk house as much as possible. By the time we were about nine, everyone knew that Mr. and Mrs. McKirk were going to get divorced, but they were desperately trying to make everything okay for their three kids. Blair had an older and a younger sister and the McKirks were more concerned with making sure their kids were not damaged by the divorce than they were with hating each other. It meant that there wasn't a lot of fighting in the house anymore, but instead there was this oppressive atmosphere of conciliation and pacification. It was a great source of treats and you could get away with almost anything at Blair's, but we all felt it. It was just wrong.

Even before things broke down for the McKirks I hated eating over at Blair's. There were just too many people. Mrs. McKirk's sister lived ten minutes away, and she and her family were over more often than not. There would sometimes be ten or more people at the dinner table, all of them talking at the same time. It was like feeding time at the zoo and I was some poor visitor who got locked in after closing time.

I only went over there a few times, but each time it was the same. A wall of noise as everyone talked at once, some cousin braying with laughter, Blair's uncle drinking beer after beer and getting louder and louder. It didn't help that Mrs. McKirk couldn't cook anything that didn't come with microwave instructions. The only good thing was that with so many people it was easy to leave the table early and hide out in Blair's room. After the divorce he got a PlayStation and his own TV. We spent hours playing *Twisted Metal*, clowns shooting as we drove our tanks into each other. You could still hear the noise from the dining room over the video game soundtrack.

If it was the Wild West at the McKirks', the Hoeffer house was like a morgue. Angela's parents were both professors at the university, and I sometimes wondered how two stereotypical bookworms could have produced a hellion like Angela. She was the first to pick up a frog, the first to jump her bike over the creek and the last to be the voice of reason on any of our adventures. Her parents looked like the most exciting thing they'd ever done was break the spine of a book. Secretly, I wished my parents were more like them. I doubted they ever forced Angela to "go out and be with people."

But dinner at the Hoeffers' was no fun — it was more like going to school, but you're the only student. Every bite was punctuated by some question about your interests, what books you're reading and what course you think you'd like to take. I wondered if Angela and her brother Tony had to answer those same interview questions when they didn't have company, too. The only upside was that it was quiet.

It was quiet at Johnny's house, too, if you don't count the noise from the TV, which was always on. It wasn't that Mr. and Mrs. Frazier ignored us, exactly; they just let us fend for ourselves. The good news was that nine times out of ten we'd get to have pizza for dinner when we were at Johnny's. The downside was that it also meant we probably had to deal with Johnny's little sister, which at best meant watching some dumb kids' movie on the VCR and at worst meant cleaning up puke.

I always tried to get out of it, but with two parents whose jobs required shift work, I was at someone's place to eat a couple of times a month until I was old enough to take care of myself. I learned to make Kraft Dinner when I was eleven and by the time I was thirteen I could roast a chicken and vegetables without help. For me, like for the ancient humans, learning to cook was a survival skill.

IT'S NOT THAT JOHNNY, BLAIR, ANGELA AND I stopped being friends in high school. We bussed in to the same school in the city and we chatted on the bus ride, but once we arrived at the enormous building in town we were individuals again. Looking back, it seems like we stopped hanging out the first day of grade ten, but it probably took a few weeks to drift apart. The high school was huge — there were more than five hundred kids, and we soon learned that it wasn't cool to hang out with kids from your neighbourhood anymore. As we got older and met more people, I think we figured out that we really didn't have that much in common.

It was strange to watch them change, from a distance but also up close. We never had a big falling out. We all still saw each other on the bus in and out every day. The conversations diminished and after a while were more often than not just brief nods before disappearing into books or Walkmans.

Johnny had finally filled out his big body with a personality to match. Sometime in the tenth grade he picked up a scary sense of humour and a voice that could have easily come from one of Blair's cousins. In the eleventh grade he was getting all the character parts in the drama productions and had even taken up singing. I can't be sure, but I'm pretty sure he was the first of us to lose his virginity, too. Girls love those drama guys, I guess.

Angela was still wild, but not in the way high school girls usually run amok. She wasn't dating university boys like Blair's sister did, or even ripping off designer jeans from the Bay. Angela, true to form, had her own style of craziness.

Blair watched Angela. He ran track, played lacrosse and in a weird turn of events had a shockingly great year as captain of the debate team, but what I noticed the most was him pining for Angela from a distance. Some things never change.

As for me? I discovered the internet.

WHEN I WAS IN HIGH SCHOOL, if people had told me that before I was thirty years old I would carry a device in my pocket that would let me talk to anyone on the planet, read the newspaper, do a crossword and take photos, all while being the greatest mix tape the world has ever seen, I would never have believed them. Who would have? We were only just getting email and the internet back then; you needed a landline phone connected to a home PC, and even that was like magic.

But fast-forward only a decade and a half, and you'll find me casually reading the X-Campus online on the john, Rogue and Magneto flipping past under my fingers as if it were the most natural thing in the world. So when the familiar jangle of the theme to the British comedy *The IT Crowd* broke my concentration, I was somehow unprepared for the shock of finally talking to my mother.

The caller ID was unfamiliar, but I was never one to screen my calls. In hindsight, sitting on the can was probably the exact situation for which voice mail was invented, but without thinking I swiped my finger over the screen, obliterating the X-Men to the interstitial space where photons and IP packets live while they wait for some device to render them sensible to human eyes.

"Brian Guillemot," I answered with my name, not knowing who was calling. It was a habit I'd picked up from work, especially helpful since pretty much no one in this part of the country could pronounce my last name. I always found it strange, since most people still took French in school, but you'd never believe the bizarre variations I'd heard, even after I'd corrected them. *Ghee-moh.* It's not that hard.

She must have paid attention when I said it, though, because she got it right. First try.

3
BREAK AND ENTER

AS IT IS FOR EVERYONE, high school was a tough time for me. No longer having the buffer of being part of a group, I was forced to navigate the dangerous sea that is adolescence alone. It could have been worse: I wasn't one of the outcasts who act as the negative to everyone else's idea of a positive self-image. No one stuffed me in a locker, beat me up or stole my gym shoes. Instead, I was pretty much universally ignored.

The old gang had split up and I knew better than to try and insinuate myself into their new circles. I'd rather have died than try out for drama club, so Johnny's pals were out. I had no chance of ever being a jock. All my life Mom had periodically tried to interest me in a game of catch or Frisbee, but I was like Dad. Kind of clumsy and entirely mystified by sports in general. I went to a few of Blair's lacrosse games, but I never figured out exactly what they were doing. The only thing I understood was a ball in the net was a goal, which was good.

And then there was Angela. She never really had a group as such, that I can recall. She'd hang out with anyone who was doing something interesting, and she somehow always managed to pull it off. The few times I tried to talk to someone who didn't already have me on their approved list of acquaintances, it was made pretty clear with various degrees of politeness that I should please fuck off. That never seemed to happen to Angela.

I think it was because everyone realized, without ever admitting it out loud, that she was the most interesting person in school.

She first got noticed a few months into tenth grade. The summer between middle school and high school she'd decided to take up rock climbing. That probably would never have led to anything except that after she'd gotten bored of the wall at the local climbing gym, she climbed the school. It was a Saturday, so she might never have gotten caught, but there was a football practice that day so the entire football team, including Coach Martinson, saw her scaling the west wall of the school.

The school was brick and had lots of sticking-out bits for her grab onto. She'd brought all her gear and supposedly was all set up with the lines and everything. They say that the coach was so impressed with her that he let her make it all the way to the roof before he started yelling at her. I don't know for sure what happened after that, but the story that went around was that she took her time rappelling down the wall, taking her gear out slowly and carefully. When she got to the bottom, Martinson was hollering at her in his booming voice but she hardly paid him any attention. She packed up her gear and stood quietly waiting for him to shut up. Supposedly when he finally stopped for breath, she said, "The rules say we can't go into the school after hours. There's nothing about going *onto* the school," and then just walked away.

I don't know if most people believe the story, but I think it went down pretty much like that. Angela always had balls.

I COULD HAVE BORROWED SOME OF ANGELA'S COURAGE in high school. As the invisible man, I didn't have a lot of friends. By eleventh grade I mostly just hung out with John Park, this guy who was deep into computers. He had his own machine, which was hooked up to the internet, and he used to spend hours surfing Yahoo! for interesting stuff. By interesting stuff, I mean hideous personal webpages made by other guys just like John, full of starry sky backgrounds and animated gifs. At the time, it was awesome.

John showed me how to access some genealogy pages and I was hooked. I knew that this was the thing I'd been waiting for my whole life, that this World Wide Web was the key to me finding my real parents. I just had to figure out how to do it.

I'd already learned that the Ministry of Children and Family Development was the government department in charge of adoptions. I'd found the paperwork in my mom's filing cabinet in her office one night when she and Dad were both working. I knew that the cabinet was Off Limits. Years before, Mom had made it very clear that police business was not for my prying eyes.

"I have official files in that office, Brian," she told me in her *Do you have any idea how fast you were going, sir?* voice. "I'm bound by the Privacy Act to ensure those files are kept secure. If I find out that anyone has been in those files, it exposes not only that person but me as well to criminal charges." I was probably rolling my eyes at this. The whole cop thing ceased to be cool once I got into middle school.

"Brian Harlan Guillemot." She raised her voice without yelling. Even at age twelve it was still scary as hell. "Do you understand what I am saying here?"

"Yeah, Mom," I sulked back at her, refusing to admit that she was freaking me out. "Don't go into the filing cabinet. I get it, okay?"

"Good," she said and smiled. "This isn't like trying to find the Christmas presents," she added. I felt my face get hot. I didn't know that she knew I'd found her stash a couple of years before and had been sneaking peeks ever since. "It's serious and I need to know you will respect this."

"Jeez, Mom," I said, desperate for this conversation to be over. "I said I get it, okay. I won't go into the filing cabinet. Promise." She didn't look convinced, but then again, she never did. Cop.

I kept that promise for four years.

The lock on the filing cabinet was pretty pathetic. As I was jimmying it open with a bent paperclip, I had to wonder about the Saanich Police Department's budget. If this was the best they could do for such sensitive files, how secure was the local jail? When the lock popped open and I rolled out the top drawer, I realized that I'd been had. I'd already figured out that Mom wasn't above dissembling a little to make her points. It was frustrating as hell, since I got the book if my parents caught me out in a lie. But Mom's filing cabinet didn't hold a single sensitive police document. It was stuffed with boring crap like birth certificates, the passports we'd gotten for a trip to Mexico, the deed to the house. And my adoption papers. The gold mine I'd been hoping for when I embarked on this B&E spree.

My hands were shaking when I realized what I held. I'm not sure exactly what I expected to find — names, addresses, photographs even? I was so nervous that I forgot to be embarrassed when I started to cry after reading over the papers and finding nothing but a registration number and some legalese. I felt like I was going to throw up. There was nothing there. I stared at the papers for a long time, then finally came to when I heard a car outside. I snapped to attention and stuffed everything back in the filing cabinet. I shut the drawer and made a vain attempt to relock the cabinet with the paperclip.

I barely made it back to my room before my dad came home.

I HAVE TO GIVE MY MOM CREDIT FOR ONE THING: she didn't get mad at me when she found the filing cabinet with its broken lock. I was so stunned by the lack of information on the documents that it took me days to realize there was no way I was going to get away with my little episode of domestic espionage. She had been in her office a bunch of times and must have seen the filing cabinet. At the time I thought she was just embarrassed about being caught in a lie about the police documents. I sometimes forgot that my mom had feelings just like the rest of us.

She never did say anything directly about the filing cabinet.

It was maybe a month later, when we were out shopping at the big-box stores on the edge of town. I had been asking for a computer of my own for months and we were on what Mom called a "fact-finding mission" to the computer shops. She'd asked a bunch of questions as if she were interrogating the sales clerk, and made the face that I knew meant she thought they all cost too much, so we left to go to the office supply place. I was sulking in the pens aisle when Mom came over with one of those accordion file boxes.

"What do you think of this?" she asked. I just shrugged and turned back to the mechanical pencils. "It's time you had your own files, Brian," she said. "You should have your passport and birth certificate and stuff. Your Social Insurance card and the adoption papers. You're going to need those things soon and you'll need somewhere to keep them."

I stopped breathing for a second, carefully not looking at her. After I regained control of myself, I picked up one of the fancy pencils with the metal casing. "Can I get this, too?" I asked. She took it from me and didn't even look at the price.

"Sure," she said, her voice uncharacteristically soft. "Why not?"

IT'S NOT LIKE WE NEVER TALKED ABOUT THE FACT that I was adopted. We just never talked about my real parents. It's like with other kids: they never talk about the fact that their parents had sex. You all know that's what happened, but you pretend it's not because it's just too embarrassing. With us, I think it was that Mom and Dad were afraid I was fantasizing about my real parents being so much better than they were. And of course, that's exactly what I was doing. Hell, even kids who aren't adopted have that fantasy. Why shouldn't I?

By the time I actually found my birth mother, I knew better. No one who is rich or famous gives up a kid for adoption to a couple from Saanich. My real parents weren't circus performers, astronauts or rock stars. They weren't even really my parents. They were just the people who screwed each other and got knocked up and didn't get an abortion. Cynical as I was by then, though, I was glad I was already sitting down when I heard her voice tentatively say, "Brian? Oh, how nice it is to finally hear your voice. This is Kim. Kim Heinz. We talked by email a few weeks back, I don't know if you remember. I'm your ... ah, well ..."

"I know who you are," I said.

4
QUESTION AUTHORITY

AFTER MY PARENTS HANDED OVER my adoption papers, it was like I was living in a dream. Not the kind of dream that is so awesome you never want to wake up. More like the kind of dream where everything is in slow motion and you feel like you could almost figure out what was going on if you could just turn around fast enough, but then you never do. I was sure that I would be able to find my real parents any second now that I had the paperwork, but nothing seemed to happen.

Of course, there was no identifying information on the adoption order itself. It was just a legal document showing that S. Holmes and D. Guillemot were now the legal parents of Brian Harlan Guillemot born April 17, 1981. I spent hours over at John Park's, surfing the web for sites geared toward kids looking for their birth parents, but they were all sob stories and no data. The government had a program to help, but you had to be over nineteen to apply. It was maddening.

When I wasn't looking over John Park's shoulder at his terminal, I was doing okay at school and watching my old friends from a distance. Johnny was almost unrecognizable in his new uniform of black jeans and black tee shirts. He still liked to eat and was no skinny emo boy, but the weight looked good on him now. He had no shortage of girls hanging around, that was for sure.

One time he invited me to one of the cast parties for the show he was in. I'd been helping him in chemistry and I think he thought it would be only fair. After the show I got a ride with him and a brace of his drama friends to this girl's house out at the edge of the city. I didn't even know whose house it was, but it seemed like half the school was there. I don't know where her parents were, but I never saw them. I did see bottles of beer and wine and vodka, plus several joints, being passed around.

I had a couple of tokes, but knew better than to try anything else. My mom had a nose for booze like you'd never imagine and I knew that the pot smell would fade well before I got home. Besides, I'd caught my dad with a joint the summer before, so I figured I could get away with the occasional hoot.

The party was strange. The people who'd been in the play were unbelievably hyper. One guy took off all his clothes and ran around the yard reciting his lines from the show. The female lead got so drunk that she spent an hour passed out in the bathroom; when she came out she started to sing show tunes. It was kind of surreal. I talked to a bunch of the people there. No one knew who I was, but when I said I was Johnny's friend, they were so nice it was like we'd been friends forever. It was probably just the beer and the pot, because when Monday rolled around they ignored me as usual.

Still, it was fun to hang out with the cool kids for a change. I was in the kitchen, drinking water and eating Cheetos, listening to a bunch of girls talking. It took a long time to realize that they were talking about Angela.

"She was in the mall downtown," a girl who wore about a pound of black eyeliner was saying. "You know, on the bottom floor, where the checkerboard is?" Her friend nodded. "And she just sits down on the floor, like there's nothing strange going on. She takes this thing out of her bag, you know those stands you use to paint a picture ..."

"An easel," her other friend said, passing around a bottle of cheap red wine.

"Yeah, a portable easel," Eyeliner said after taking a healthy slug from the bottle. "Anyway, she sets this thing up in front of her, calm as can be, then puts a canvas on there. Then she starts to paint, some kind of abstract thing, I think. I mean, she's not painting a picture of the mall. There's no reason she has to be there: she just acts like no one can stop her. She sits there for like an hour, just painting her weird picture."

"What about Security?" one of the girls asked.

"They didn't do anything!" the storyteller said, incredulously. "I mean, can you imagine getting away with that? But I don't think she even thought it was weird to be sitting on the floor of the mall painting a picture. I mean, she's just like that. She just does whatever she wants and doesn't even realize how bizarre it is."

"I think she's awesome," someone said.

"Yeah," the girl telling the story said after a pause to stare at the wine bottle. "Angela's authentic. A real authentic life." There was no small hint of envy in her voice. We'd been reading the existentialists in English class and everyone was desperate for authenticity that term.

"Angela's always been that way," I heard myself say, and the group turned to look at me. I'm not sure they even knew I was there until I spoke.

"You know her?" Eyeliner asked, disbelief all over her face. I just shrugged.

"She's my neighbour," I said. "We used to ride bikes when we were kids."

"Cool," one of the girls said. "What's she like?"

"I dunno," I said. "She's just Angela."

"Yeah," someone said, like I'd just said something profound. "She is Angela. Like, really *is*, you know?"

"Totally," someone else said and passed the wine bottle my way.

I shook my head and said, "See ya," then walked out of the kitchen. It was getting late and the last bus back out to the boonies was going to leave soon. I found Johnny in the basement with a bunch of other people, playing spin the bottle by the look of things.

"You bussing back home?" I asked.

"Yeah," he said.

"We better go, then," I said and waited while he hugged everyone goodbye. Johnny did a lot of hugging.

As we rode the bus up the peninsula, I told him about the story the girls in the kitchen were telling about Angela. He laughed.

"She was always her own person," he said.

"That she was," I agreed, wondering exactly what that meant. "Johnny, do I smell like weed?"

I WASN'T A POTHEAD BACK THEN, but I smoked. Everyone did. They say that the biggest industry in the province is BC Bud, and if the Island was anything to go by, it's probably true. Even Mom didn't care that much about the odd joint. Cops wouldn't bust you for smoking; they only cared about the grow ops in junked-up old houses. Doubtless, if she'd caught me with a bag of weed I'd have been in major trouble, but even though possession was still illegal, no one got arrested for it.

So it was that I was out smoking a joint in the woods by my house when I ran into Angela. It was maybe a month after the party with Johnny's friends and I was still surprised both that I'd had a good time at the party and that no one had talked to me after. I heard a rustling in the trees and hastily put out the joint. I was trying to hide it in this little Ziploc bag when Angela burst into the clearing where I was sitting.

"Heya, Gumbo," she said, grinning. "You smoking a jay?"

"Yeah," I said, my face colouring. I don't know why Angela catching me with a joint would be embarrassing, but it was. "You wanna toke?" I asked.

"Sure," she said and sat down on the log next to me. I sparked up the joint and, after sucking down a hit or two to get it going, passed it over to her. She took a couple quick tokes, held the smoke in her lungs, then passed it back. We spent a few minutes smoking in silence. Then she said, "Heard you were at that party at China Smithers' house."

I frowned. "Johnny took me to the cast party for *Guys and Dolls* a few weeks back," I said. "Never knew whose house it was, though."

"Yeah, that's it," she said. "How much fun was that?" She grinned and I wondered what she knew.

"It was okay," I said, shrugging. "How come you weren't there?"

She frowned. "No one asked me," she said. "I don't hang out with that crowd too much," she added.

"They seem to like you plenty," I said.

"What makes you say that?" she asked, suspicion in her voice. I wished I hadn't said anything.

"Oh, you know ..." I said, hoping she'd drop it, but Angela never dropped anything like that.

"Come on, Gum," she said. "Spill it."

"Just some people talking, you know," I said. "About you painting at the mall. They all thought it was pretty cool."

She frowned. "That was months ago," she said finally. "It was raining and I needed decent light. You know my house is dark as the devil's asshole." She had taken to creative cursing. It was just another aspect to her mystique. "So, what's so great about painting in the mall?" she asked.

I shrugged. "Everyone thinks you're a real individual," I said. "At least Johnny's crowd does."

She laughed, but it didn't seem like she found anything funny about what I'd said. "So individual that I couldn't possibly want an invitation to a party, eh?"

I looked over at her. "I think they're scared of you, Ange. I bet if you just showed up, they'd be beside themselves to hang out with you."

"Yeah, whatever," she said, looking off into the trees. "Any luck on the parents thing?" she asked. It was no secret from anyone except Mom and Dad that I was looking for my birth parents. I mean, who wouldn't be?

"Not yet," I said. "I can't do much until I'm nineteen."

"That's such bullshit," she said, fire in her voice. "Too bad your mom's such a bully." Angela wore a bright yellow button on her army surplus backpack that read *Question Authority*, and she often did. She'd taken to calling them fascists: cops, teachers, whoever tried to tell her what to do. My mom was not immune to Angela's anger.

I was used to it, but I didn't know what she meant. "If it weren't for your mom, your dad would probably just tell you who your parents are. He's such a sweetheart." Everyone knew my dad was the biggest softie in the neighbourhood.

"I don't think they know," I said. "It's not on any of the forms and I looked it up. They don't tell the adoptive parents anything about the birth parents unless it's an open adoption. Which it wasn't, or I wouldn't be looking."

"Come on," Angela said, exasperation in her voice. "Sherlock could find out if she wanted to." With that, she stood up and headed back out of the woods. "Thanks for the smoke, Gumbo. Hang loose."

MY MOM WAS SADDLED WITH THE UNFORTUNATE NAME of Shirley Holmes. It might not have been so bad if she hadn't decided to become a police officer, but the nickname was obvious and impossible to avoid once she did. She could have taken Dad's last name when she got married, but that wasn't her style. I'm still a little surprised that she didn't make him change his last name to hers, or worse yet, hyphenate them.

But thankfully I wasn't stuck with Holmes. I guess it was growing up with Mom's annoying nickname that made me immediately think of ketchup when I heard my real mother's voice on the phone that morning.

"Kim Heinz," she repeated.

"It's good to finally hear from you," I said. "I've been look-ing for you for a long time."

"Well," she said. "Here I am."

5
BUSH PARTY

BY THE TIME I WAS IN TWELFTH GRADE, I'd resigned myself to the fact that I just wasn't getting anywhere with finding my birth parents on my own. Once I was nineteen, I could access my records and register with the government. Then, if my birth parents also registered, there was a possibility we could connect. It sounded so easy, but I tried not to get too hopeful. These were the people who gave away a newborn baby, after all. It wasn't hard to imagine a scenario where they wouldn't be all that interested in being found.

So I focussed on my schoolwork. I somehow developed a real non-parents-related interest in John Park's internet and finally managed to convince my parents to buy me a computer of my own. I played up the educational aspects of it: accessing the university library, reading about advances in science and technology. I think they thought I just wanted it to play games, and there was plenty of that. But I actually had gotten interested in science and spent an awful lot more time than you'd expect a seventeen-year-old to spend at the webpages of NASA and MIT.

I applied to the engineering programs at UBC, Simon Fraser and UVic. Like everyone else I knew, I'd have given my right nut to go to Vancouver for school. When you're seventeen years old, living on the Island is like living in the boondocks, only more so. You know everyone, everyone knows you and the good bands never come to your town to play. Vancouver was like Las Vegas, Paris and New York all rolled into one. It was only a couple of hours away by ferry, but it was still far enough that going over was a major undertaking. And, of course, it was expensive.

Which was why I knew it probably didn't matter whether or not I got accepted to the Vancouver schools. Although in all the discussion, wheedling and arguments about it, I found that I had a surprising ally in my petition to move to the mainland for university.

"It would be good for him to gain a little independence, Dom," my mom said to my dad one night when we were hashing it out again for the billionth time.

"What does that even mean, Shirley?" Dad countered. "He could buy a beater car for less than it would cost to live in res. That's more independence than he'd have being stuck with the bus in Vancouver."

"Guys," I said, "I'm sitting right here."

"Sorry, Brian," Mom said.

"And what about all the crime?" my dad continued as if no one else had said anything. "Gangs, junkies ... it's not safe over there."

"Dom," my mom said, "it's not as bad as it sounds. It's a big city, there's a lot going on every day. Of course you hear about it when something bad happens, but really it's just as safe as Victoria on a day-to-day basis. Besides, UBC is in the middle of nowhere, relatively speaking."

"Exactly," Dad said. "Living in res means Brian would be practically as far away from the city as he is now." He turned to look at me. "And anyway, it's a moot point," he said with finality. "We just can't afford it."

And that was the gist of the problem. My parents had started saving up for my education the day they signed the papers, and there was just enough to pay for four years — if I lived at home. Even with summer jobs, there was no way I could make up the difference for rent, even in residence. And it would be hard to get a student loan just because I wanted to be in the big city. Plus, even I knew enough to realize that I'd be better off without a big chunk of debt when I left school.

And so even though we probably wasted a night or two a week for my entire twelfth grade year fighting about it, there was never really any question about it. I was going to the University of Victoria or nowhere.

WHEN I GRADUATED FROM HIGH SCHOOL, there was this enormous bush party out near Blair's place. It wasn't just for those of us out on the peninsula; the whole graduating class was invited, plus probably an equal number of other kids. Older brothers and sisters, kids from other schools, the odd eleventh grader who was particularly cool. The after-grad party was the party of the year.

In something of a tradition, the older kids always got the booze for the party. We had to pay for it, of course, and I suspect that they made a bit of a profit off us, but it was worth it. The cops turned a blind eye to the whole thing — underage drinking, drinking in public, the copious amounts of pot going around.

The week before the party, my mom sat me down. "I don't want you to lie to me about what goes on at the after-grad party," she began, and I gulped. "So I'm not going to ask you anything. If anything happens that you think you want to tell me, then I'll listen, but otherwise I trust you to be smart about things." She looked out the big picture window that faced into our yard. She seemed almost sad, but I couldn't imagine why.

"I know there's going to be drinking, and ... other stuff," she continued. "And I don't expect you not to have a beer or two. Just be careful, be safe. Don't get into a car with anyone who's inebriated, and stick to the party. Every few years some kid goes off in the bush and ends up falling down a ravine or something. I don't want that to happen this year and I especially don't want it happening to you."

I didn't have anything to say during this bizarre un-cop-like talk we were having. Finally, she said, "I'm proud of you, Brian.

You're a good kid and you deserve to have a little fun. I know it's hard for you, me being a police officer and everything. So just go and have a good time, okay?" She smiled, and I could almost see that there was someone under there who wasn't all bound up in the uniform. Almost.

Dad had less to say, but it was just as awkward. He handed me fifty dollars and a brand-new box of condoms. "Just in case," he said and grinned while I just about died. When I was in middle school, he had spent an afternoon putting condoms on bananas and cucumbers with me while telling me about sexually transmitted diseases. As a nurse, he had a scary number of stories about young guys with gonorrhea, herpes and even HIV. It was mortifying, but I was the go-to source for condoms for years. Dad made sure there was always a full box in the bathroom, and he handed them out to me and my friends like he'd never handed out candy. It was horrible and awesome at the same time.

The party was surreal. I only remember snatches of it now. I drank more than I'd ever drunk before, trying to make the most of my mom's free pass. I remember puking behind a stand of trees in time to the music playing on someone's portable CD player. I remember sitting by the fire, mesmerized by the yellow and red sparks, having a deep and meaningful conversation with someone whose name I don't think I ever knew. And, remarkably, I clearly remember being successfully and entirely seduced by Jacquie, Blair's older sister.

I'D NEVER REALLY TALKED TO BLAIR'S SISTER BEFORE. She wasn't much more than a year older than me — Blair was one of the younger kids in our grade — but she'd graduated two years before. She was sophisticated, she'd been around and she was gorgeous. Looking back on it, she was probably just reacting to their parents' divorce, but she was known to be a man-eater. And I'd somehow shown up on her list of possible meals.

I don't remember how we got to talking, but I remember her handing me the first of many vodka coolers — the downfall of many a teenage drinker. They taste like candy and pack a boozy wallop. After a few of those, I found myself following her into the trees, her hand in mine pulling me through the shrubbery. I don't think I had any idea what was coming, though honestly I don't think things would have happened any differently if I'd had a week's advance notice.

We broke into a small clearing and all of a sudden she was on me. Her mouth on my mouth, hot and wet, her tongue snaking into my mouth. It was momentarily paralyzing; then my drunkenness and eighteen-year-old hormones took over and I was making the most of the situation. My hands went all over her and she didn't do anything to stop me. It didn't take long before I'd gotten her shirt off and one of my hands down her jeans. I was so busy that it took me a second to realize what she was doing with her own hands.

I'm still amazed that I managed to get one of the condoms out and on in time. It was over almost as fast as it had started, but even with everything that happened after, I still remember it fondly. It was the first time I'd ever had sex and it was the last time for a long time that I ever did it without a tiny rush of panic. It wasn't all Jacquie's fault, but I blamed her for years. What Jacquie giveth, Jacquie taketh away.

IT WAS JULY. SUMMER WAS IN FULL SWING. I was working at the A&W and hating every second of it. I couldn't wait for the summer to be over so I could start university. I'd even managed to get sort of excited about going to UVic. I was on a break at work one afternoon when I heard Jacquie's voice from the next booth over.

"I missed my period," I heard her say.

"Who's the guy?" her friend asked.

"Just a friend of Blair's, it's no big deal."

"You've told him, though, right?"

"No, he doesn't need to know. I'll deal with it."

Somehow, I found myself in the staff bathroom; I don't remember getting up from the table. I stood there in the john, red and black spots before my eyes. I had to sit down with my head between my legs for five minutes before I could breathe again. I knew exactly what that meant. Jacquie was pregnant and it was my fault.

In the days that followed, the phrase *Like father, like son* kept going around and around my mind. This is exactly what my dad, my real dad, must have felt. Terrified. Like his life was over. Like nothing worse could ever possibly happen.

"SO YOU LIVE IN VICTORIA?" Kim asked, even though I'd told her all that in the email.

"Yeah," I said. "You're up island?"

"Near Maple Bay," she said. My heart fluttered. Maple Bay was only about an hour's drive away. Maybe some weekend ...

"But I'll be coming into Victoria next week," she continued and I felt as sick as I had overhearing Jacquie's conversation all those years before. "Maybe we could get lunch?"

6
THE THING WITH JACQUIE

I DIDN'T TELL ANYONE ABOUT JACQUIE. What would I say? Who would I tell? My parents would be so disappointed. I didn't even want to imagine the look on my dad's face. Johnny was worldly enough, I thought, but I didn't know how to casually call him up and say, "Hiya, buddy. I haven't talked to you since that party last year, but I've knocked up Blair's sister. Any idea what I should do?"

Obviously, talking to Blair was out. I thought he'd probably murder me for just screwing around with Jacquie; I didn't want to think about what might happen if he found out about this. Angela might have understood, but she was gone tree planting for the summer. John Park and I never once had a conversation that didn't involve computers. So there was no one. It was just me and my dread.

It wasn't surprising that Mom and Dad noticed something was up. I never could tell a lie, and just not saying anything about this felt like a massive whopper. About a week after I overheard Jacquie's conversation, Mom was still at work and Dad was making a batch of his famous ribs for dinner. The meat was boiling on the stove while he mixed up his barbecue sauce, and I was quietly fretting at the dining room table. "What's on your mind, Gumbo?" he asked. He only ever used my nickname when he was trying to be especially nice to me.

"Nothing."

"You seem a little preoccupied lately," he said, licking the wooden spoon and pursing his lips. He reached for the bottle of hot sauce and as he dripped tiny amounts into the bowl said, "I remember when I graduated from high school. It felt so great, like I was finally free, like I was finally an adult. But then that feeling faded and I started to really freak out about what I was going to do with my life. I mean, I didn't know what I wanted to do." He stirred the sauce and put the spoon down. He turned toward me and grinned. "Well, that's not entirely true. I knew I wanted to smoke joints, drink beer and get into Madeleine Zaworsky's pants."

"Dad!" I said, momentarily shocked out of my funk. He just laughed and poked at the pot of ribs.

"Oh, come on," he said, "I wasn't always old and boring. I remember being eighteen perfectly well. And I know that it's not all fun and games, either. There's a lot of pressure on you right now, more than there was on me at your age. Kids these days are expected to have it all figured out: school, career, the whole bit. I just want to let you know that I'm here for you if you want to talk. You don't have to decide your whole life right now, you know."

"Thanks," I said and wished to hell that declaring a major was the worst of my worries. I gave Dad a weak smile and went out to the yard to light the barbecue.

I STILL HADN'T HEARD FROM JACQUIE. I was too scared to call her, but I knew that I had to talk to her. I wasn't ready for this, not by a long shot, but I was going to take responsibility. Whatever that meant.

I had some money saved up from the A&W job; I figured I could probably pay for an abortion with it. I knew that it was up to her, though, so I looked into maybe getting some construction work instead of going to school. There were plenty of unskilled labour jobs available and they paid pretty well.

I thought I could support a baby on those wages. I tried not to think about the other option. No one would expect me to marry her, would they? I mean, it was almost the twenty-first century. Right?

At the back of my mind I knew there was more to fatherhood than financial support. But it was too big, too oppressive to really contemplate. I was only eighteen. I still felt like a kid myself. How could I be a father now? It was like a giant weight was sitting on my chest, invisibly crushing me.

I walked over to the McKirks' one afternoon when I figured that Mrs. McKirk would be at work and Blair would be at soccer practice. I didn't know Jacquie's schedule, but I assumed that in her delicate condition she wouldn't stray far from home. I hoped their little sister Debbie would be at camp or something.

I got to the big yellow door at about three in the afternoon and could hear the sound of talk-show television from the rec room. I couldn't see in, but I hoped it was Jacquie. I rang the doorbell and waited. The TV noise continued, but I couldn't hear anyone moving around. I rang again, waited some more, then walked around to the back door. I could see through the window that a couple of people were in the rec room. I could smell pot and after a minute I heard Jacquie's loud laugh.

I banged on the back door and heard a male voice curse. After a few minutes, Jacquie came to the door. Her shirt was on wrong and her jeans were undone. "Blair's not here," she said to me, her eyes bloodshot.

"I'm not here for Blair," I said softly.

"Hurry up, baby," I heard the guy call from inside the house.

"Just a sec," Jacquie hollered back. "So what do you want?" she said to me.

"We need to talk," I said.

"We do?" she said.

"Yeah," I said, "about, you know, the baby?" I was starting to feel my heart rate increase and I had to fight with my legs just to keep standing there.

Jacquie looked puzzled for a moment, then said, "Oh, shit, how do you know about that?"

"I overheard you with your friend. At the A&W."

"Jesus, Brian, it was just a false alarm. I'm not pregnant, you idiot."

I must have looked like someone slapped me, because she burst out laughing. "Serves you right for eavesdropping." She shut the screen door and I could hear her laugh fading as she walked into the house.

I WALKED AWAY FROM THE MCKIRKS' IN A DAZE. My feet moved on their own and took me into the woods where we'd played as kids and now we went to drink, smoke or screw. I wasn't even looking where I was going; I was literally blind with rage. I always thought that was just a saying, but it turns out it's real. I've probably never been as angry as I was that afternoon. It took hours before I even started to feel the relief that eventually poured over me like a breaking wave. And when it did finally come, I was glad I was on my own, in my favourite clearing in the woods, because I cried so hard that I thought I was going to throw up.

I barely made it home in time for dinner. I caught Dad giving me funny looks all night, though by then I was just so happy that I wasn't going to be anyone's teenaged father, I didn't care about anything else. I ate three helpings of scary vegetable surprise and even consented to play Scrabble with Mom and Dad, although it was cheap Tuesday at the movies.

After I got a triple word score with *reinstate*, I remembered Dad's little talk from earlier that summer. "I'm not worried about school," I proclaimed to my parents without preamble. "Engineering's a good course, I think I'm going to like it and there are lots of jobs for gearheads. I'm going to be okay." I said the last sentence like it was some kind of prophetic pronouncement. Then I grinned at the two of them like an idiot and went back to my letter tiles. "Is there any potato salad left?" I asked as I shuffled the Q, Z and H I'd just drawn.

I'M SURE THAT IF IT HADN'T BEEN for The Thing with Jacquie I might have been more concerned with starting university. I had done pretty well in high school, but I had heard that engineering was killer. The rumour was that they failed out something like thirty percent of the freshman class, and there were definitely brainier kids out there than me. But being pre-occupied with The Thing with Jacquie, then with the sense of being suddenly pardoned off Death Row once there no longer was a Thing, I let university kind of creep up on me.

The same feeling of being startled by something you'd watched approach for ten miles hit me when I heard myself say, "Lunch would be great. I know a good place downtown, quiet but very nice."

"I'm a vegetarian," Kim said, a tone of apology in her voice.

"No problem," I said. "They do lots of veggie things there. And there's parking," I added, immediately cursing my banality.

She thankfully ignored it and said, "Great. What's the address?"

"I'll email you a map," I said, and the phone fell from my sweaty hands and clattered to the bathroom linoleum.

7
YOU'VE GOT MAIL

AFTER I GOT OFF THE TOILET, I didn't know what to do. I wandered around the apartment in a daze and finally snapped back to reality when I found myself in the kitchen washing the already clean dishes. Feeling like an idiot, I drained the sink and dried off my hands. I fired up my laptop, got a Google map of the place I'd picked out for lunch and a dorky headshot of myself, and sent them off to kheinz@pawznclawz.ca. I managed to include what I thought was a more sane-sounding note than what I'd said on the phone, full of safe platitudes like how much I was looking forward to meeting her.

After I sent the email, I picked up my phone and started to call Beth. We'd met at an adult adoptee support group, but I'd stopped going after we broke up. I figured she was there first, and my need for support was less than hers at this point. But I really wanted to talk to someone, someone who understood how fantastic and terrifying meeting my mother was. Beth would understand.

"What do you want, Brian?" she said, her voice hard. We hadn't spoken in weeks and the last time hadn't exactly been pleasant.

"I'm meeting Kim in a few days," I said.

"Well, isn't that nice for you," she said.

"I just wanted your opinion," I said, hoping we could get

past meanness and just talk, like we used to. "You always had the best ideas, the best strategies. Come on, Beth, I'm just looking for help here."

"Yeah, I know," she said, no trace of friendliness in her voice. "That's all you ever wanted from me. Someone who understood how hard it is to be poor little Brian Guillemot. Well, I'm done with that now. You got what you wanted, you got your contact. You don't need me anymore and I sure as hell don't need you. I hope you and your mother have a lovely time and I never see you again."

She hung up.

I was stunned. She was so bitter, so angry, even though it had been her idea to break up. I looked dumbly at the phone in my hand. I would never understand women. Never.

I THOUGHT THINGS WOULD BE DIFFERENT WITH BETH. I always think things will be different. How else could I ever even go on a first date if I didn't believe that? Beth was really promising, though. She understood about being careful. She really understood. I thought.

When we met at the group, we hit it off right away. We'd had all the same questions throughout our childhood. Her adopted parents were a nice couple from the mainland who'd been unable to have kids of their own and adopted Beth when they were almost in their forties. Growing up with older parents had its own issues. According to Beth, they were more lenient than her peers' folks were in some ways, but had some strangely outdated ideas in other ways. Beth grew up with no restrictions on where to play or with whom; her parents let her run around their suburban Vancouver neighbourhood unchecked. She got almost any toy or trinket she asked for, and they even let her eat ice cream for breakfast on weekends.

When she got into high school, though, Mr. and Mrs. Soderberg changed. They wouldn't let her hang out with her friends unless there was a specific activity planned. "In my day," her mom would say, "we didn't just walk the streets. Is that what you want? To be a streetwalker?" Beth thought her mom was only kind of kidding, as if hanging out with a bunch of other teenagers at the mall would inexorably lead to a life of drug addiction and prostitution. "Penury is probably what she would have called it," Beth once said. "I kind of think they believed that bad behaviour could be passed along genetically. Like they were just waiting for me to get knocked up myself."

She wasn't forbidden to date, exactly, but her parents wouldn't let her go anywhere without an itinerary and a plan of how she would get there and back and exactly when. It made dating tough and just hanging out impossible.

Otherwise, though, Beth loved her parents, just like I love mine. But she was always haunted by the question of who her birth parents were.

WHEN I STARTED GOING TO MEETINGS of the Adult Adoptee Support Network, I was feeling as disillusioned with the parent search as I ever got. It had been five years since I had paid my two hundred and fifty bucks to the Adoption Reunion Registry for a search, and all I'd ever gotten was a single name: Wilhelmina Heinz. You'd think there wouldn't be that many Wilhelmina Heinzes to go through before I tracked down the one who was my birth mother. And you'd be right, there weren't many. It's just that none of them were her.

I'd spent hours searching Canada411.com and PeopleFinder. com, looking for W. Heinzes. Most of them were Williams and none of them were Wilhelminas. The people at the government agency looked, too, using whatever secret government spy tools they had. They got nowhere either. I received a nice letter informing me that "all search procedures have been exhausted" and that my file "would be placed in inactive status." The letter promised that "should additional information become available, the file would be reviewed." It read like every other Please Fuck Off letter I've ever gotten.

I was out of ideas. I'd known about the Support Network for a couple of years, but I'd never been desperate enough to hang out with a bunch of other sad cases looking for mommy and daddy. After my file was "placed in inactive status," I became exactly that desperate.

THE MEETINGS WEREN'T AS PATHETIC as I'd imagined they might be. Mostly, we talked about search techniques and occasionally one of the members would strike gold. Then we'd talk endlessly about reunions, the need to be sensitive to others' discomfort, how to pick neutral ground ... everything we'd all secretly fantasized about for as long as we'd known we were adopted.

I asked Beth out on a date after the fifth meeting I attended.

We went to a very nice Italian restaurant downtown, where they take no reservations but give you free cheap red wine in coffee cups while you wait in line. We spent a very enjoyable evening getting quietly sloshed on wine and talking about everything other than being adopted. We already knew about that part of each other's lives, so it seemed pointless to rehash it.

Beth worked in a bank as some kind of manager. I never really understood it and she never really explained. It was the same with my job. We left work at work, and when we were together we talked about other things. Soon enough, the adoption issue no longer was off limits and we spent a lot of time comparing search strategies.

Focussing on a single name was Beth's idea and I have to give her all the credit. I'd had no luck with Wilhelmina Heinz, so Beth suggested I try each of the names separately. It wasn't a strategy that would ever have worked for her: her birth mother's name was Susan Jones. But my mother's names were unusual enough that it might have worked.

I knew that I had been born in Victoria, and there was only one hospital with open records for this sort of thing. I sent an official request for information on women admitted to the maternity ward in April 1981 with the first name of Wilhelmina. Six weeks later, I got a nice answer telling me that there were no Wilhelminas admitted at that time.

My hopes dropped. I'd managed to convince myself that this was it, this was the way I could finally track her down. When I got the letter, Beth talked me out of what certainly would have become a month-long funk. "Try Heinz," she said. "There really aren't that many of them. It's worth a shot." So I did.

And there she was. W. Kimberly Heinz. My mom.

IT WASN'T AS SIMPLE AFTER THAT AS I'D HOPED it might be, but once I gave up on all the Wilhelminas it was just a matter of time. I wrote a nice letter to N. Frantzman, the name at the bottom of the PFO from the province, and provided N. with the new information needed to reopen my case. Miraculously, the department really did reactivate my file and in late July 2010, I got the letter I'd been waiting my whole life to get.

The only thing I even saw when I opened it was a strange line with an improbable number of instances of the letter Z: kheinz@pawznclawz.ca

HOW DO YOU SEND AN EMAIL to the mother you've never met? Is there some modern etiquette book for situations like this? What would it be called? *Emily Post and the Etiquette of Twenty-First-Century Family Dynamics? So, You've Got Two Mommies,*

So What? I think there's a market here. Someone could do well with this book.

As much as I wanted to make contact as soon as possible, it took me nearly a week to finally send my mother an email. I must have gone through twenty drafts.

```
Dear Ms. Heinz,
I got your email address from the
Ministry of Children and Family Services,
as part of an adoptee parents search. I
believe that it is possible that you and
I may be related.


To W. Kimberly Heinz:
I have been searching for you for a long
time. Please reply to this email.


Are you the Wilhelmina Kimberly Heinz who
gave birth to a baby boy at the Victoria
General Hospital on April 16, 1981? If
so, please reply.


Hi.
You don't know me, but I think I'm your
son.
```

BETH HELPED A LOT. She practically wrote the final version that got sent and when I got an answer she cried. "I'm so happy for you, Gumbo," she said, though I thought she didn't sound exactly happy. "This is wonderful."

Ms. Heinz — Kim, as she asked me to call her — replied quickly, I'll give her that. I don't know what I was expecting: shock, fear, wonder, an outpouring of emotion. But I wasn't expecting to get the response I got. I'm not complaining, but it was kind of overwhelming in its totally normal tone.

hi brian

its good to hear from you. ive been
wondering whatever happened to you and im
glad you turned out okay.

im kinda busy with the store and the
new birds i took home but we should
get together sometime. give me your
phone number and ill call. dont freak
out if you dont hear from me for a few
months, im a big flake but ill get there
eventually! ha ha.

cheers
kim

THE DAY I GOT THE EMAIL, Beth wanted to take me out to dinner to celebrate. We went to the same restaurant we'd gone to on our first date; it was where we always went for special occasions. Things were great over the appetizers, but by the time half my plate of seafood pasta was gone, Beth was drunk and crying softly into her eggplant parmigiana. We skipped dessert and I took her home.

I got her into her apartment and into bed. She was a wreck and I wasn't sure why. I waited while she fell asleep, then went back to my apartment. It wasn't much of a celebration after all.

I should have seen it coming that night, but I was so sure Beth would be different. Over the next three weeks we couldn't seem to stop arguing.

We had The Fight about a month later.

8
PAWZ N CLAWZ

O, THANKS TO BETH, I was on my own. No problem. I'd
only spent most of my online life reading forums, blogs
and personal pages about adoptees meeting their birth
parents. I could probably write a dissertation on the subject.
Somehow, all that research didn't seem to be helping. My stomach was roiling around like a drunken octopus, and my heart
would have formed a perfectly usable drum background to any
punk rock song. Be careful what you wish for.

For probably the billionth time since I got the letter from
Children and Family Services with Kim's email address, I
surfed to pawznclawz.ca. It was the website for a pretty eclectic pet store up island, where her email address indicated that
Kim worked. They had the usual puppies and guppies, but
they seemed to specialize in exotic birds. Their site was pretty
rudimentary — I wondered if they'd updated it since 1999, the
year they opened.

Obviously, I'd been hoping for a staff photo gallery. Lots
of small business websites have them: people like to see pictures of people. It's a proven marketing technique. Pawz N
Clawz didn't seem to know about it, though. Their site had a
few photos of the store, badly lit and poorly composed shots
that seemed to show off the cages much better than the animals they contained. On the other hand, they also had some
great pictures of some of the individual animals. There was

a particularly adorable chocolate brown puppy I could easily have taken home with me if I weren't allergic.

And then there was the bird gallery. These people obviously lived for birds. I don't know what most of them were, but there was an amazing variety. They were green and blue and red and yellow; big and small and tiny and enormous. They had scary-looking talons with razor-sharp beaks and delicate little feet with tiny little heads. I can only imagine what that place sounded like when they all got going. I wondered how many of them talked.

I still can't tell you exactly what it is I thought I was going to learn from scrolling through the photos of birds. If she worked there, maybe my mother had a thing for birds herself. She'd mentioned birds in her email to me. I'd read it over several thousand times and I could recite it word for mispunctuated word. I guess I wanted a little clue to what she was like. More than knowing that she was a self-professed "flake" who believed that email didn't require the same level of writing skill as other forms of written communication. At least, I hoped she didn't write like that all the time. But for all I knew she was functionally illiterate. Maybe she cleaned the cages at Pawz N Clawz as part of a government job program for disabled people. I had no idea what I was getting myself into at Café Mozart.

WE'D AGREED TO MEET ON SUNDAY at one o'clock. I usually spent Sunday afternoons with Mom and Dad, drinking beer, eating barbecue and avoiding talking about my life. I called them to cancel on the Tuesday before, hoping to get the machine.

"Hello," my dad's voice boomed out of the phone, cheery and energetic. Wincing, I turned the volume down.

"Hi, it's me."

"Oh, hi," he said, his voice quieter but somehow even cheerier. "I didn't expect to hear from you. What's up?"

"I can't make it for dinner Sunday," I said.

"Oh, that's a shame," he said. "Is everything okay?"

"Yeah," I said. "Just something came up."

"Okay," he said, then with a sly tone asked, "is it a woman?"

"No," I said, then backpedalled. I didn't tell my parents a lot about my life, but I was a terrible liar, so I tried not to say anything actually untrue. "Well, yeah," I corrected. "But it's not what you think."

"Huh," he said. "Now you've really got me curious."

I took a deep breath. I knew I was going to have to do this sometime and it seemed like now was the time. "I've found my birth mother," I said. "We're meeting for the first time on Sunday." There was a very long pause on the other end of the line. "Dad?" I asked. "You there?"

"Yeah," he said, finally. "I'm here." Another long pause, this one I didn't interrupt. "She found you?"

"No," I said, knowing he didn't just hear me wrong. "I found her."

Another pause. Eventually, he said, "We didn't know you were even looking."

"You must have thought I might," I said, unable to believe that he and Mom hadn't known something. "How could I not want to know?"

"Sure," Dad said. "It's only natural. I'm just surprised, that's all. You never said anything." All the life and energy that had been in his voice when he'd picked up the phone was gone. It was like I was talking to a different person.

"Come on, Dad," I said, trying to be kind. "I didn't want you and Mom to feel bad, like I was, I dunno, trying to replace you or something. It didn't seem like something you talk about with your parents."

"I guess," he said. "You know you can always talk to us about anything." It sounded like one of his many lectures when I was growing up. "Even this. Especially this." He sighed. "Your mother and I always expected you'd be curious. That's why we gave you all the papers and things when you were a teenager. But you never said anything about wanting to find your birth parents, and some kids, well, they just don't want to know. We finally figured that you were one of them." He took a breath. "It's just a surprise, is all."

I didn't know what to say. "I'm sorry," I finally said, feebly.

"No," he said. "You don't have to tell us, though I'm glad you finally did. I hope it goes well, your meeting."

"Me, too," I said.

"If you feel you'd like to," Dad said, "we'd like to hear about it. But it's up to you. This is your thing, not ours."

"Thanks, Dad," I said. "I don't know ..."

"It's okay," he said. "Just know that your mom and I love you. No matter what."

"I know, Dad," I said. "I love you guys, too."

"We know that," he said. "We know."

I GOT TO THE CAFÉ AT ABOUT A QUARTER AFTER TWELVE. I hadn't planned to be so early, but I was so nervous that I couldn't stay in my apartment any longer. I'd finally gotten up at six a.m., after lying awake for what seemed like hours. I didn't think I'd ever been this nervous before — not for a job interview, not for a date, not even when I walked over to Jacquie McKirk's and found out she wasn't pregnant after all. For a while, I thought I was going to throw up.

Café Mozart is, I think, one of the best-kept secrets in downtown Victoria. It's a two- or three-minute walk from all the major office buildings, yet on a weekday noon hour there's almost always a table available. They do okay there, but it's off the beaten path so it's never as busy as the other eateries in the main business district. But their food is fantastic. I have to ration myself so I don't eat there every day.

It's some kind of European/Californian/Asian fusion thing they've got going on. Lots of quiches, soups, rice and noodle bowls and enormous grilled sandwiches. Plus there's always a special, some kind of really substantial meal. In the years I've gone there I've eaten everything from spanakopita to an eggplant and chèvre stack and once even pork chops with apple sauce.

Sundays were no busier than any other day, so I slid into a table near the window as soon as I arrived. I ordered herbal tea in the hopes of calming my nerves, and it arrived in a huge cup with a small almond cookie on the saucer. I smiled at the waiter and sipped the tea.

Getting there early didn't calm my nerves much, but the tea and cookie helped. I spent the time surfing the internet on my phone and staring out the window. *Is that her?* I wondered about the haggard-looking brunette fighting with the parking meter across the street. *What about her?* the short, chubby lady talking on the phone by the door. I was staring at a bleached-blonde woman about the right age, who had a Dachshund in one of those tiny dog carriers disguised as a giant handbag, when I felt a presence at the table.

I looked up to see a short woman with close-cropped dark hair and a broad smile. "Brian?" she asked. She stuck her hand out for a shake. "I'm Kim."

9
CAFÉ MOZART

SHE ORDERED FALAFEL AND BABA GHANOUJ, a fact I remember more clearly than the beginnings of our conversation. I think it stuck in my mind because it was such a bold choice — foreign and garlicky and made for sharing. It put my black forest ham and gruyère panini to shame. A part of my mind was amazed that I was focussing on the food at this of all times. The rest of me was just trying to get through the moment.

After we had plates between us to buffer the awkwardness of meeting, the small talk receded and we actually talked. Between openly delighted bites of her meal, Kim gave me the basic outline she thought I wanted.

"I was sixteen years old when I had you," she said, idly mopping a piece of pita bread in the spicy eggplant dip. "I was in high school and there just wasn't any chance of me keeping a baby."

I nodded. "I can completely understand that," I said, flashes of The Thing with Jacquie in my mind. Kim seemed to notice something on my face, because her face took on a little smile of recognition. "Sixteen is young," I added.

She nodded. "It is," she agreed. "And with my parents, there wasn't much else in the way of options." She shrugged. "Honestly, if it had been up to me, you might not have made it. But it took me a long time to realize that I was pregnant and by then my mother had put two and two together herself. Mom and Dad are ..." She paused, her dark eyes aimed at the ceiling, as if some explanation for the strangeness of all parents could be found in the acoustical tile at Café Mozart. "They were crazy Christians before being a crazy Christian was cool," she said finally.

I didn't know what to say to that. "Your parents were strongly religious?" I prodded.

"True, but that's not the best way to describe it," she said, a sad smile on her face. "You know those nutty Americans, the ones down south, who play with snakes and speak gibberish and have those terrifying television programs where they heal the lame and cure the sick?" I nodded. "Well, that's how I grew up. Only back in the seventies, it was my folks and, like, three other families in the province who did this shit.

"We were just lucky that there was no such thing as home-schooling back then, or me and my brother would be total fruitcakes ourselves, I'm sure. As it was, it didn't take long for me and Wolf to figure out that Mom and Dad were nuts. We just had to play along until we were old enough to get out." She ate another bit of falafel and when she was done chewing said, "Lucky for you, I got knocked up a couple years too soon."

I don't know why I was so shocked. That Kim had a less than perfect childhood, I'd been expecting, even if the details were weird. But it never occurred to me that she'd sit across from me, eating pita, talking about why she didn't get an abortion. I'd thought of it, of course, many times. I knew it had to have been something she considered. I think I just never thought I'd hear her say it out loud, as if it were the same as getting a mole removed.

I recovered somewhat and changed the subject. "It must have been very hard for you, pregnant so young and with such a religious family."

She shrugged. "By then my parents had already consigned me and Wolf to hell. We were doomed just by not believing the claptrap they tried to shove down our throats. The rest of our sinning behaviour was just icing on the cake." She stopped and turned to look at the café's counter. "Hey, cake! Wanna share a slice?"

She was far too casual about this. I know not everyone is as serious as I am, but cake? Really? What could I do? I said, "Sure," and Kim waved down our waiter to order a slice of the chocolate torte.

"When I got pregnant, I think they were expecting it. Not because I got around, they wouldn't have known one way or another about that, but because it was just the kind of thing a child of Satan would do. I think they are eternally disappointed that Wolf is a lawyer, rather than serving out life for some heinous crime." She shook her head, laughing slightly.

"It seems like you had a rough time of it," I said.

"I'm giving you a very one-sided picture of what it was like growing up," she said. "Ninety percent of the time, Mom and Dad were pretty normal parents. They took care of us, we always had food and clothes and they really valued education. They paid Wolf's way through law school and would have sent me to college too if I'd wanted it. They offered to raise my child — to raise you — when it happened. But I figured that you'd be better off with someone else, someone who really wanted you, who really wanted to be parents."

The cake arrived and she took a giant forkful. Closing her eyes as she ate it, she laid the fork along the side of the place. "So tell me about them," she said when she'd swallowed. "Your parents."

I gave her the short version — cop, nurse, nice, loving, kind of weird. She nodded and I added, "They've been great parents. I can't complain and lots of kids really can. I just wanted, you know, to know where I came from."

She nodded. "I understand. I've wondered about you all these years. Every time I got pregnant — I have three other kids — I thought about you. And now that we've met, I'm glad I made the choice I did. You seem to be a good man and your parents sound like a better set than mine were." She looked into my eyes and said, "Don't ever forget, Brian, it's easy to have a child. It's not so easy to raise a child. And the two aren't really related at all."

"So," I said, toying with the last crumbs of the cake. "You have other children ..."

"Yeah," Kim said. "Charlotte, Rob and Jeannette. Charlotte's twenty-six, Rob is twenty-three and Jeannette's just a baby at eighteen."

I did the math. "So, you got married when you were nineteen or twenty?"

She shook her head. "I've never been married," she said. "Once I left home, I kind of let myself just be free, you know? I lived with Aaron, Charlotte's dad, for a couple of years, but it didn't last. Rob's dad was just a big mistake." She made a *What was I thinking?* face. "I stuck around with Chris the longest. But we grew apart and Jeannette was, like, ten when we split up. Relationships are tough."

"Yeah," I said, wondering what it must have been like for those kids. I couldn't really imagine it; even when the McKirks got divorced, they just fought and then Mr. McKirk moved out. It's not like there was some new guy in the house every few years. I fought not to judge her. It did, however, open the door to one of the questions that had been burning in the back of my mind.

"Speaking of which," I said, as nonchalantly as possible, "I'd been hoping you might give me a lead on my own father. I'm hoping to meet him someday, too."

It seemed like a cloud passed over Kim's face and all the casual cool was gone from her demeanour. "Don't hope too hard, kid," she said.

"Well, I'd still like his name," I pressed.

"I don't like to talk about it," Kim said, staring fixedly out the window.

"But ..." I started, and she cut me off with glare.

"Don't push it, Brian," she said. "I'm really glad we're connecting here, but this isn't just your show. I said I don't want to talk about it, and I mean it. Not now. Maybe not ever. And that's final."

I nearly said, "Okay, Mom," in a sulky teenage voice. Instead, I looked out the window, feeling lost.

We were silent for a few moments; then Kim smacked her hand on the table. The soft slap broke me out of my trance and I looked over at her, startled.

"You should come out to the house next month," she said, all trace of her earlier coldness gone.

"Uh, okay," I said.

"Charlotte's getting married in August and all the kids are coming over to hang out at my place in July. I have an acreage and there's room for camping and stuff. It's sort of like a family reunion." She looked at me and grinned. "And what a great time for you to meet your half-siblings! A family reunion, indeed. It'll be great."

"I, ah," I stammered, completely dumbfounded by this turn of events. "Sure, I guess," I said. "You're talking like a couple of days?"

"Sure," she said, "or a week or two, whatever. It's pretty free and easy over at my place. You have a tent?" I shook my head. "No matter," she said. "We can figure something out. An extra body is never any big deal." She looked at me and beamed. "It's going to be great!"

She pulled her wallet out of her purse and started toting up what she owed. "No," I said, "it's my treat, please."

She smiled and said, "You sure?" I nodded and she put her wallet away. "Well, that's awfully nice of you, Brian," she said, then looked at her watch. "Damn it, I've got to get a move on." She stood, and I stood, and we awkwardly looked at each other for a moment. She finally came around the table and gave me a quick hug.

"It was good to meet you," she said, smiling. "I'm glad you tracked me down. Now, I really hope you get a chance to come up while the kids are all there. It's going to be a laugh." She slipped her sunglasses on and walked to the door. She stopped and turned back to me.

She said, "I'll send you a map."

10
THE NEW KID ON THE BLOCK

T HE TINY TRUNK OF MY HONDA CIVIC was nearly filled by the tent, sleeping bag and air mattress I'd rented from one of the local outdoors outfitters. I couldn't remember the last time I'd been camping — it was probably with Johnny, Blair and Ange in someone's backyard before we'd hit double digits. Sleeping where there's nothing between you and the dirt but a few layers of nylon and polyester didn't fill me with joy. But I didn't want to impose myself on Kim too much; it was enough to be invited to this bizarre get-together as it was.

As I drove up the highway toward Maple Bay, the other cars passed me impatiently. I was a pretty good driver, I thought. I'd never had a speeding ticket and usually was pretty close to the limit. I was driving way slower than usual this morning, though. I wanted to meet my half-siblings, I really did. After all the thinking I'd done about my real parents — imagining their lives and experiences in the last thirty years — it had never occurred to me that I might have siblings.

When I was growing up, people often expressed their pity for me when they found out I was an only child. It was always odd to me. No one ever said it was a shame I was adopted — I guess that would just be too politically incorrect to say aloud. But a shocking number of people — other kids' parents, teachers, friends of the family — told me what a pity it was that I didn't have a brother or sister to play with. Mom and Dad always let it slide, which struck me as kind of cowardly. I knew it was their choice to adopt only one kid; after one of these comments they had mentioned it. They should have stuck up for their decision, especially because I thought it was a good one.

It's not like I was never lonely or bored as a kid. I had lots of those days. But I never once wished for a brother or sister. I liked being the sole object of my parents' attention when I was young, and by the time I was old enough to wish there was someone else to deflect their scrutiny, I'd known enough kids with siblings to see that they were obviously more trouble than they were worth. Even Johnny Frazier, who got along pretty well with his sister, was constantly having to stay home to take care of her, or share his toys, or some other pain-in-the-ass thing. I just never saw the attraction of a brother or sister.

And now it turned out that I had three of them. Two sisters and a brother. What would they expect from me? Anything? I wondered whether they would be interested in meeting me, or just annoyed at me barging in on their family. Would we get along? Would we even have anything in common? We certainly had very different childhood experiences. I couldn't stop thinking about what they would be like.

An angry car horn shocked me out of my musings and I realized that I'd been going sixty in an eighty zone as a U-Haul truck sped past me. I wasn't paying any attention to the road and that was a recipe for a crash. I shook my head, turned up the stereo and tried to focus on driving.

I DON'T KNOW WHAT I WAS EXPECTING. I think I had some kind of idea of a sixties-era free-for-all, with camper vans and tents scattered willy-nilly on overgrown brush. I pictured animals of all kinds running free alongside dirty, feral children. I had the phrase *white trash* in my mind and with it an embarrassed feeling of combined superiority and guilt. I guess it was the combination of the word *camping* along with prejudices about unmarried women having children that I hadn't known I'd fully formed. I knew I was being unfair and offensive, but I couldn't seem to shake it. It made for an uncomfortable feeling.

So, of course, I was surprised to find a tidy ranch house on a large lot, with a couple of tents pitched in an orderly fashion among a grove of trees. There was a single large RV parked near the house and a bunch of people hanging out in the yard by a picnic table. It reminded me most of my own parents' house on a Sunday afternoon when they'd invite some of the neighbours over. Shame washed over me like hot waves of nausea.

It took me a moment to get out of the car, and a young woman about my age managed to notice me before I could get myself together. She had very short dark hair and was dressed in what I called Mountain Equipment Co-op chic: tan quick-dry trousers made of some space-age material and a light-coloured, short-sleeved plaid button-up shirt. I couldn't see her feet, but I guessed that her shoes would be either hiking sandals or chunky walking shoes.

"Mom," she bellowed toward the knot of people in the yard. "The new kid's here!"

SHE TURNED OUT TO BE CHARLOTTE, and I was right about the footwear: she wore a sturdy pair of surprisingly bright red shoes. I introduced myself when I got disentangled from my seat belt and out of the Civic.

"Hi," I said, hoping my voice wasn't wavering too noticeably. "I'm Brian." I stuck out my hand and she took it in a firm grasp. "People call me Gumbo."

She gave a short, clipped laugh. "Nice," she said, pointedly not asking for an explanation. "I'm Charlotte. Folks call me Chuck." She jerked her head toward the mass of people by the picnic table. "Come on," she said. "I'll introduce you to the mob. They're all pretty harmless, at least at this time of day."

She grinned and I followed her quick walk back to the group.

I recognized Kim sitting at the table with a tall glass of something cool-looking in her hand, and she said, "I'm so glad you could make it." She turned to the group and raised her voice above the din of eight conversations. "Everyone, this is Brian. Brian Guillemot. Say hi." Then she sat down again and took a sip of her drink.

I was overwhelmed. Of course I was. But once I got over the initial shock of all those people, it wasn't as bad as I thought it would be. Rob and Jeannette introduced themselves to me right away, and I could see the resemblance between them and Chuck. I wondered if they saw something of themselves in me — I looked for it but didn't really find anything. Maybe something in Rob's freckles. Maybe not.

"You must need a beer," Rob said, flinging his arm over my shoulder. He was a little taller than me and had the rangy athletic build of a high school runner who still kept it up.

I grinned at him. "That would probably help," I said and let him steer me toward a huge cooler sitting on a bench near the door to the house. He opened it and fished around in the ice, pulling out a pair of Piper's Pale Ales. He held the bottles up for my approval and I nodded. He twisted off the tops with practised ease, handed one to me and clinked his bottle to mine.

"Cheers, buddy." He drank.

"Cheers," I replied, taking a sip.

"It looks bad," he said, gesturing to the crowd of a dozen or more people. "But don't worry about remembering names. It'll come eventually and until it does we'll forgive you." He took another sip of his beer. "We should've worn name tags or something." He pointed to an older man and woman talking to Kim.

"That's Uncle Wolf and his wife Barbara." He pointed his beer toward a large knot of people around my age. "Over there are their kids, June and Michael. Their other kid, Sandra, will be here later." More beer pointing. "That's June's husband Chris and Michael's wife Marita. She's from El Salvador. Great cook, makes these corn meal and beans things that are to die for. There's some on the table, you gotta try them. And they've got a pair of little ones, Isabela and Ramón. June and Chris have a baby, Suzanne. I don't know where she is — probably in the house with Michael's two. They love the new baby."

"Wow," I said. "I'm never going to remember that."

"No problem," Rob said, laughing. "Totally should have worn name tags, man."

AFTER A COUPLE MORE BEERS and a bunch of Marita's *pupusas*, I had about half the names down. I'd talked to all the adults by then, including Rob's girlfriend Anna, who had been watching the kids in the house when he'd been making the introductions.

"I'm an only child, too," she said when I'd finally met her and we found ourselves in a quiet corner of the kitchen. "So I kind of know how you feel."

"It's a bit overwhelming," I said, and she laughed.

"Tell me about it," she said. "The first, like, ten times I came to some family thing with Rob, I was a total wreck. There's just, like, so *many* of them."

I laughed. "It probably doesn't even seem like a lot of people to them," I said. "Plenty of families are a lot bigger."

"I know," Anna said. "But not mine. My parents came to Canada when I was one and I never knew any of my relatives. It was only ever the three of us. This —" she waved her hand to indicate the whole Heinz clan "— this was like meeting a bunch of space aliens. Crazy." She shook her head. "But they are all great people and they get it. That it's strange for us. They'll be cool, just take your time."

She smiled and I thanked her. I took a breath and the two of us walked back out into the yard and the melee.

"SO, ISN'T TERRY COMING, TOO?" someone, maybe Michael, maybe Chris, asked Chuck as we were all seated around the tables and tucking into an enormous barbecue dinner.

"After supper," Chuck said through a mouthful of sausage. "Work."

"Chuck got herself a librarian," Jeannette told me as an explanation. I'd already guessed from overheard conversations that Terry was the other half of the upcoming wedding. "It's a pretty good laugh for all of us," Jeannette went on.

"Why's that?" I asked.

"'Cause Chuck never read a single book in her life," she said loudly enough for her sister to hear, grinning.

"I heard that," Charlotte said from the other end of the table. "I have so read a book."

"Oh yeah?" Jeannette said. "That wasn't a mechanic's manual?"

"Sure," Chuck said, a big grin on her face. "I read a real book. Literature, even." She paused for effect. "*Zen and the Art of Motorcycle Maintenance.*"

Everyone who was listening laughed, and I got the feeling that the joke had been told more than once in the past. I laughed along with everyone else and for a moment almost even felt like part of the group.

11
SEEDY P AND THE TECHNICOLOR SCREAM

I'D BEEN A BIT OF A LONER IN HIGH SCHOOL and just assumed the same would be true for my university years. It didn't even occur to me that things might change, so it kind of snuck up on me to discover I was actually part of a group.

The first few months of my freshman year of university were mostly a blur of homework, exams and studying. I'd heard all the stories, but first-year engineering was harder than I had even imagined it could be. It was the math. Finally, an answer to that ubiquitous question: when will I ever need algebra? And not just algebra — trig, conics, even the calculus. Though I actually liked it. It wasn't hard for me to lose a couple of hours in the library studying and not even notice that the time had gone by. I had to come to terms with it: I was a big nerd.

I mean, come on. I even called it *the* calculus.

But by second term I'd discovered that nerds aren't actually the social outcasts the movies make us out to be. Pretty soon a bunch of us from engineering were regularly hanging out together on campus and, when course load allowed, off campus. When we had some free time, the guys who were nineteen would boot for us on the weekends and we'd drink beer and talk about the structural integrity of the Johnson Street Bridge or the coming Y2K crisis until the wee hours. It was a small group, but it was mine.

It was one of these guys, Tom Spindle, who managed to talk me into going to this fundraiser for some campus group — Ski Club, Glee Club — I don't remember. It was going to be a bunch of local bands with names like Aluminium Lizard and the Razorblade Roses. The thing was out in some warehouse, but the Tree Club had organized a bunch of busses from campus going out there. Tickets were twenty bucks, which I thought was kind of pricey for just local garage bands, but the drinks were supposed to be cheap and they didn't ID anyone. For me, and the three other eighteen-year-olds in the group, this was worth the jumped-up cover price.

I'd arranged to stay with Spindle for the night, since his folks were decidedly not cops about underage drinking and their house was close enough to campus for a cheap cab ride back after the last bus. It was going to be epic.

We met up on campus and caught the fourth bus out to the warehouse, after waiting in line for over an hour. Ryan Devine, the guy we figured most likely to end up in Chem E and the biggest pothead in our group, passed around a massive joint while we hung out, which took the sting out of waiting.

By the time we got to the warehouse, the opening bands had been and gone and they were already out of the decent beer. We each grabbed a pair of Luckys from the bar and elbowed our way up to the stage.

It was hot as an oven in there. I guessed that there were probably five hundred people in the place, the majority of them packed onto the floor in front of the stage. After a few beers, though, it stopped feeling uncomfortable and got pretty fun. I'd been back to the bar about three times and somehow managed to snag one or two free drinks along the way. I was wearing someone's beat-up sombrero and offering piggyback rides to all comers when the Scream came on stage.

It would be romantic to say that I was immediately transfixed as she walked up to the microphone, her torn lace dress and combat boots burning their image indelibly into my mind. I'd like to pretend that our eyes locked during the chorus of their first number and she picked me out of the crowd. But the reality was that I only barely noticed when her gruff alto filled the PA system with a guttural yell of "I'm Seedy P! And these motherfuckers behind me are the Technicolor Scream. And we're here to fuck. You. UP!"

The band pumped out a wall of noise, not entirely unlike what the previous groups had done, but Seedy P's rough but surprisingly melodious voice was a change of pace. I noticed her, sure. Who didn't? She was the lead singer of the third-last band of the night. They had played a couple of the smaller punk venues in Victoria and they had their fans. I wasn't one of them, but I thought they were okay. I stayed up by the stage until I lost the sombrero and wandered out of the crowd for some fresh air and another beer.

WE PROBABLY WOULD NEVER HAVE MET if I hadn't been puking behind the bathrooms after the gig. Spindle and I almost missed the last bus because I was still dry heaving, but he finally manhandled me into the coach before the doors slammed shut. He chucked me into a seat, and I felt myself fall into a soft person-shaped pillow. I had just about nodded off when she elbowed me in the ribs.

Somehow it sobered me up enough that I looked over to my right to see Seedy P squished up between me and the window. "Hey," she said, her voice whisky and cigarette rough.

"Hey," I said, recognition crawling slowly into my mind. "You're with that band ..."

"Yeah," she said.

"You guys are really good," I said with great originality.

"Thanks," she said. "If you're going to pass out, let's switch places, okay? I don't wanna get crushed by a drunk frat boy again."

"Sure," I said, getting up and nearly taking a header down the aisle of the bus while she slipped out. "I'm not a frat boy, though," I added, sliding into the seat. "I'm an engineer."

She laughed. "Good to meet you, Señor Engineer," she said, sitting down again.

"Huh?" I grunted eloquently. She pointed at my lap, where at some point I'd apparently tied a pair of maracas to my belt. "Huh," I said, again. "I guess they came with the sombrero." Then blackness descended.

I DON'T KNOW WHAT EXACTLY SHE FOUND ENDEARING in that exchange, but I must have made an impression. A couple of weeks later, I was reading my Applied Mathematics textbook while sitting on the grass and eating a sandwich. I felt rather than saw someone sit down next to me, and then a hand reached out to grab my sandwich, which was sitting on a bit of wax paper on top of my backpack.

"What is this?" she said. "Chicken and cheese?" She took a bite of the sandwich and chewed slowly. After she swallowed, she said, "Not bad," then took another giant bite. I still had yet to find my voice.

She wore a black tank top and a very, very short black-and-red plaid skirt, but was saved from looking even a tiny bit tarty by the thick, baggy, heavily holed black tights that filled the space between the tops of her Army surplus store boots and the hem of her skirt. She sat beside me cross-legged, grinning disarmingly, as she tried to take a third bite of my sandwich.

Hunger and indignation finally won out over shock and intimidation, and I grabbed my sandwich back from her. She laughed and picked up my textbook. "So, how's it going, Señor Engineer? You seem a little more with it today." She flipped though the textbook while I stuffed the last of my sandwich in my mouth in an attempt to take it out of circulation. "You understand any of this?" she asked, turning the book so I could see the lines of equations.

I nodded, chewing, and wondered if I was ever going to actually speak to her sober. "Cool," she said, flipping through a few pages. I finally swallowed and said, "So what does it stand for?"

"What?" she asked.

"Seedy P," I said. "That can't be your real name."

She frowned. "Uh-uh," she said. "That puts me at a distinct disadvantage, Señor. You first. What's your name?"

"Brian," I said. "Brian Guillemot. People call me Gumbo."

She grinned. "Awesome," she said and leaned in toward me. "I love Southern food. Mmmm. Spicy."

I felt my face get hot and realized that while she might just be playing with me, it was a game I was starting to enjoy. A lot. "Well," I said. "Tit for tat."

She arched an eyebrow, but didn't comment. "Fair enough. My name's Celia-Dee Pavane. Hence, Seedy P. Get it?"

"I got it," I said.

"Good," she said. "So, the Scream's playing at the bar under the Sticky Wicket this Friday. If you want I could put you on the list."

"That would be awesome," I said. "Can I bring someone?"

"You got a girlfriend?" she asked, her face stone.

"No," I said, an admission which usually embarrassed me but somehow now made me inordinately pleased. "I owe my buddy Spindle big time and I know he'd love to see the show."

She grinned at me again and said, "He's the guy nursemaided you home after the warehouse gig?" I smiled and nodded, and she said, "Okay, yeah. You owe him, all right. So it'll be Brian Gumbo plus one." She stood up, making no concession whatsoever for the fact that she was wearing a skirt. "See you there?"

"You bet."

SPINDLE DID NOT BELIEVE ME for a second when I told him that we were on the guest list for the Seedy P and the Technicolor Scream show, but he was perfectly willing to let me make myself look like an idiot. So Friday night, at nine o'clock, we were standing in the rain with about fifty other people on Government Street. When we got up to the front, I said, "Brian Gumbo?" to the monkey at the door and wished I'd had a camera for the look on Spindle's face when we were summarily waved through and our hands stamped.

"What the hell did you do, Gumbo?" Spindle said over the sound from the PA as we walked down the steps into the club. "Write an exam for her or something?" I just shrugged. "Jesus," he went on. "They didn't even ID you or anything. Who the hell are you, man?"

"What can I say?" I said as we pushed our way into the crowd of people in the basement room. "She likes me."

12
FAMILIAR ALIENS

I **LIKED KIM AND HER KIDS,** but after a couple of hours of in-jokes and multiple simultaneous conversations, I had to get away. "You don't have to work," Kim said when I offered to help with the cleaning up. "You're still new — new people don't have to clean. You get a free pass your first time." She smiled and I returned the grin.

"I appreciate it," I said, "but I didn't contribute anything else." I indicated the remains of the huge spread that had been potlucked by the group. "At least let me do this."

Rob's girlfriend, Anna, caught my eye and stood. "I'll keep him company, Kim," she said, and the two women shared a look.

"All right," Kim acquiesced, "but don't forget that it was your call, Brian. And no free pass next time, either."

MOST OF THE CUTLERY AND PLATES fit into Kim's dishwasher, and Anna and I took care of the pots, pans and serving dishes in no time. "I could see where your mind was going," she said. "Clean-up is a good way to get away from the madness for a while."

I nodded, elbow deep in the sudsy water. "They are a good bunch of people," I said. "But it was getting overwhelming again."

"Yup," Anna said. "After three years I'm a lot better than I was, but I still need my time out. Babysitting helps, but this is even better." She dried a large rectangular dish and found a spot for it on the sideboard. "So this must have been double weird for you," she said. "I mean, these folks don't actually belong to me. But you're meeting a huge number of your own family here. Must be so strange."

"It is," I said. "I wanted this for so long ... meeting my parents, anyway. I somehow never even imagined brothers and sisters. And connecting with Kim has really meant a lot to me, but ..." I trailed off.

"But what?"

"But she's ... *they* are all just people. Just folks. I don't know what I was expecting — monsters, Martians, superstars? But they feel both familiar and alien in that way that my childhood friends' families felt when I went over there for any length of time. Like it was just like being at home, only somehow different enough to be utterly baffling."

She laughed. "All families are unique and all families are the same," she said. "Just like the people in them."

Before we could continue this conversation, we heard the front door open. A soft female voice called out, "Hello?" and Anna answered back. Soon a blonde head poked through the kitchen door.

"Hi," she said. She was a little younger than me, dressed in a long, full brown skirt and some kind of flowy blouse that you might see on a buxom tavern maid at a Renaissance Faire. I thought I could even see flowers poking out of her hair.

"Hiya," Anna said and leaned over for a quick hug and kiss. "This is Brian Guillemot," she said, turning to me.

"They got you working already?" the new woman asked, laughing.

"I volunteered," I said. I went through a process of elimination on my mental list of attendees. "You must be Wolf's daughter, Sandra."

She and Anna shared a glance; then she frowned almost comically. "No one bothered ..." the putative Sandra said, then stopped. "No." She turned to me. "I'm Terry. Terry Frost. Chuck's girlfriend."

"Oh, I'm sorry," I said, uttering the classic Canadian statement required in any awkward or uncomfortable situation, then recovering. "Congratulations on your engagement."

"Thanks," she said me, then turned to Anna. "Those jerks."

"I don't think it was on purpose," Anna said. "I never thought to mention it, either. I guess I just assumed someone said 'she' at some point."

"It's no big deal," I said. "All anyone said about you was that you were a librarian and the best thing that Chuck ever brought into the house."

"Well, isn't he a charmer," Terry said to Anna, then turned to head toward the back door. "This family gets better with every new addition, don't you think?" And with that, she walked out to the yard.

THE SUMMER SUN WAS STILL POKING OVER THE HORIZON, but the kids had all been packed off to bed and a fire was roaring in the brick-lined pit. I wasn't much of a nighthawk and could feel my body starting to shut down. Still, I wasn't ready to crawl off to my rented tent just yet. Thankfully, I'd had the presence of mind earlier to wrestle it from the trunk of the Civic and find a spot in the yard to put it up. Jeannette had seen me struggling and came over to help.

"Is this even your tent?" she asked skeptically as I was leafing through the dog-eared instruction pamphlet and staring at the various items that came out of the package.

I shook my head. "Rented," I said. "I'm not a big camper, you know?"

She nodded and picked up the bits and pieces that had fallen to the ground. "Yeah," she said. "They had me pitching my own tent by the time I was seven. I can do it in the dark now."

"I appreciate the help," I said as I watched her expertly set up the small portable shelter.

"No problem," she said, hammering the stakes into the ground with a stick. "So, I don't want to be rude or anything..." Her voice faded off.

"Ask your questions," I said. "I'm surprised that no one wants to talk about my situation."

"Everyone's curious," she said. "They're just too polite." She grinned at me. "It won't last."

I laughed. "So what do you want to know?"

"What was it like?" she asked. "Being adopted?"

"Huh," I said. "That's hard to answer. I mean, what's it like not being adopted? It's just the way things were. I mean, it had some strange advantages and disadvantages, but everything in life is a tradeoff."

"Like what?" she asked.

"Well," I said, "when I found out how babies were made, I never had to imagine my parents actually doing that." We both laughed. "And when they did something totally embarrassing, I had the luxury of knowing that we didn't share any genetic material, so I had a chance not to turn out crazy like them. Stuff like that."

"And they really wanted you," she said, looking away.

"Yeah," I said softly. "They did."

We were quiet for a moment. Then Jeannette asked, "So, was there this big *there's no Santa Claus* kind of drama when you found out?"

"No," I laughed. "I don't know when they told me; it must have been when I was little. It feels like I've always known. But they were really weird that way."

"What do you mean?" she asked.

"They never did the whole Santa Claus, Easter Bunny thing," I said. "They were into honesty with me. It was almost like they didn't treat me like a kid, or at least they didn't treat me like I was dumb. It was cool, in a way, but kind of awkward, too."

"Being the only kid who knows the truth about Santa could be tricky," she said.

"That was only the half of it," I said, thinking back. I sat down on a tree stump. "Want to hear a funny story?"

"Sure," she said.

"Okay, so my dad's a nurse. In our house we always used the proper terms for body parts and illnesses and whatnot. I must have been the only eight-year-old who tried to get out of school by complaining of gastrointestinal distress." She laughed. "Anyway, there was this one time in third grade. My friend Blair was kind of a brat, and at recess this one day he's bragging to all the other boys that he showed Julie Hopkins his dinkus. Everyone is really impressed, of course. I don't know what the hell he's talking about, but I don't want to be left out of something cool. So what do I do?"

She shrugged, leaning in for the punchline. "I ask him if I can see it, too." She burst out laughing.

"You're a funny guy, Gumbo," she said. "And not just funny ha-ha, either."

"Thanks," I said. "I think."

"You'll fit in here just fine."

AS WE SAT BY THE FIRE, the night drawing in upon us, the novelty of my arrival in the family seemed to have worn off. Everyone was talking about the ancient and well-worn topics that fill family get-togethers without going out of their way to include me, and that felt more normal than the endless explanations and translations earlier had been. I could feel myself getting more and more tired, but it was nice just to be comfortably ignored in the group, so I stayed longer than I might have.

They'd explained that in the morning, the "kids" — my generation — usually had a big breakfast together, while the "grown-ups" — Kim, Wolf and Barbara — took care of the little ones. I took the explanation as an invitation and as I stood to pick my way to my tent, I tapped Rob on the shoulder.

"I'm in the little blue tent over by the big tree," I said. "Don't let me miss breakfast, okay?"

"No problem, buddy," he said. "I'll get you up in time."

I found my way to the house and used the bathroom, then fought with the complicated opening to the tent for a while before I finally breached its defences. I crawled into the tiny space and got into the sleeping bag. I had only enough time to think that I could get used to these people before I fell into a deep and dreamless sleep.

13
THE BIRD WHISPERER

THE MORNING CAME QUICKER than seemed at all reasonable. I was awoken by Rob's voice loud outside the tent. "Hey, Gumbo," he called. "Get up if you wanna eat."

I had a moment of panic as I found myself tangled in the unfamiliar sleeping bag. Once I located the zipper and extricated myself from the down-and-nylon coffin, I felt my heart rate decrease and my sense of alertness start to grow.

"You look like you could use a cup of coffee," the real Sandra said as I made my way into the kitchen. She'd arrived while we were at the fire pit, and Rob had introduced us.

"Thanks," I said and accepted the large mug gratefully. She pointed me toward the fixings, and I doctored the coffee quickly before taking a sip. "Just what I needed," I said and sat at the large round table that dominated the kitchen.

Chuck was mixing up a huge bowl of pancake batter while Rob and Jeannette tag-teamed a griddle of eggs, bacon and dollar hotcakes. Pretty soon the table was loaded with an assortment of morning-after breakfast foods, and the eighteen-to-thirty-five-year-olds were gathered around it, putting short work to the lot.

After we'd all had a round of protein, carbs and grease, Terry asked me, "So, how was your crash course into this crazy clan?"

"Fantastic," I said with only a small amount more enthusiasm than I really felt. "You guys have been great. I never expected to be so welcomed. It's kind of amazing."

"Well," Rob said, "it's something we all wondered about, too. We all knew about you — Mom never kept it a secret that she'd given up a baby for adoption."

"It's the cornerstone of her birds and bees talk," Jeannette said. "Mom's never been shy about using her choices as examples for the rest of us."

"So you've known about me all your lives," I said, feeling the heat of embarrassment starting up. "Wow. That's kind of ... I don't know."

"We aren't exactly the Cleavers," Rob said. "We aren't even the Simpsons. An extra kid out there we'd never met was hardly the strangest thing we all had to deal with growing up."

"Yeah," Chuck said. "Don't forget we all have different dads and there were times when that was mighty damned complicated."

"I can imagine," I said. "So, what are they like?"

"Our dads?" she asked.

"Yeah," I said. "You've all met your dads, right?" I hoped I hadn't started a conversation no one wanted to have with a stranger.

"Oh, yeah," Rob said, grimacing. "They've all been around at one time or another."

"My dad lives in Vancouver," Chuck said. "After they split up, I used to part-time it between here and there. I went to school here and summered over there — it was kind of backwards, but Van in the summer can be a blast. My dad's okay. He and Mom just were too young, probably. It's not exactly like me coming along was part of the plan, either."

"I see my dad all the time," Jeannette said. "He lived here with us when I was a kid. Now he's got a place in Victoria."

"Chris is a good guy," Rob said.

"He's okay," Jeannette said with somewhat less enthusiasm.

"How about you?" I asked Rob, after he didn't jump in at the natural point.

"My dad's an asshole," he said simply. "I haven't seen him since I was fifteen years old, and as far as I'm concerned that's just fine." He didn't seem to want to say any more and I didn't press it. No one else disputed his statement either, so I guessed there was something to his assessment.

"So," I began after a pause, "did Kim ever mention anything about my father?"

Before anyone could answer, I heard a scream from deep in the house. "What the hell?" I said, dropping the bit of toast I was still toying with, and half standing. "Who is that? Is everything okay?"

"Did no one give him the tour?" Terry asked the rest of the table. They all looked at each other with blank looks and shrugs. "You people are terrible," she said with mock exasperation. She stood and said, "Fine, I'll do it. Come on, Gumbo. Let's go meet the birds."

THERE HAD TO BE A DOZEN OR MORE OF THEM. Everything from a little budgie in a cute little gold cage to a giant green-and-red squawker sitting on a branch in some kind of giant parrot house. "It's an aviary," Terry said. "Sort of the bird equivalent of an aquarium."

The windows had been darkened when we walked into the room, but Terry opened the blinds and that somehow turned on the audio of the occupants. Shrieks, squawks and chatter filled the room, almost to deafening proportions. It was unlike anything I'd ever encountered.

Terry took me on a brief round of introductions. "This is Peter Piper," she said, pointing to a big grey bird in its own cage. "He's kind of scared of strangers." I was waggling my fingers on the bars of the cage when in a grey streak the bird flew at me, beak and claws flashing. I jumped back and Terry said, "I'd keep my fingers away if I were you."

The bird seemed to scowl at me as I passed by, and I swore it growled at our closest point of approach. "This is Suzie. Hiya, Suzie," Terry cooed at the cute little pink-and-yellow songbird.

"She's a pretty one, aren't you, Suzie Q?" The bird opened its beak and a thin, reedy choke came out. Terry turned to me and said, "She's the grand dame of the group. Kim's had Suzie and another one, Roscoe, since she was eighteen. Parrots live forever. The rest of them are pet store rejects."

"Seriously?" I asked.

"Yup," Terry said. We continued around the room, meeting birds with some defect or another that kept them from being saleable. Most of the parrots were mean or crazy, and the other birds were all healthy but in some way not desirable as pets. "Squawk," the giant red-and-green parrot in its own aviary said to me as we approached.

"This is Napoleon," Terry said, a smirk tugging at the corners of her mouth.

"He's the emperor here, is he?" I asked.

"Not Napoleon as in Bonaparte," she said. "More like Dynamite."

"Squawk," Napoleon said. "Idiot. Idiot. Squawk."

I laughed. "I'm amazed they couldn't sell him," I said. "I can see lots of people finding that hilarious."

Terry nodded. "Yeah, the talking is fine," she said. "It's the biting and scratching that's the problem. He's a great chatter and singer, but nasty as all hell. Ole Peter back there is a pussy-cat by comparison. You really don't want to get anywhere near Napoleon; Kim's the only one who can get into his cage. He'll scratch your eyes out, given a chance."

"Good to know," I said, looking at Napoleon out of the corner of my eye. We left the bird room and the chorus of noise quieted but didn't stop as we closed the door.

BACK IN THE KITCHEN, CHUCK EXPLAINED. "The store has contracts with a bunch of bird breeders and they get regular shipments in. The birds are often too young to have fully developed by the time they arrive at the store, so some bad behaviours just don't manifest until it's too late. They could send the bad birds back — it's what most stores do — but the birds would probably be destroyed. Mom isn't about to allow that, so we end up with all the bad birds here."

"She's got a knack for them," Rob said. "When I was a kid, Mom spent hours training me with them. I'm okay with the birds, but nothing like her. I tried to feed Napoleon once and nearly lost my hand. Mom seems to never have a problem. It's a gift, though I sometimes wonder how useful being a bird whisperer really is nowadays."

"How many birds are there?" I asked.

"Sixteen?" Jeannette said. "Maybe more."

"And there are a pair of dogs," Chuck added, "a bunch of cats and —" she turned to Jeannette "— is the hedgehog still here?" Jeannette nodded. Chuck turned back to me. "All of them at the store are a bunch of sucks for animals, but Mom's the biggest softie of the lot. We've had at least one of everything they sell over the years — spiders, snakes, iguanas, ferrets, you name it."

"But more birds than anything," Jeannette said. "Mom loves her birds." More coffee was poured around the table and we sat in companionable silence for a moment. That was when I remembered what we'd been talking about before the birds had interrupted us.

"So," I began again, not knowing how to get back to the topic I desperately wanted to discuss without seeming to be, well, desperate. "You'd all been telling me about your dads before. Did Kim, um, ever say anything about mine?" I hid in my coffee cup, but still noticed the awkward looks going around the table.

Finally Jeannette said, "She won't talk about it. It's, like, the only off-limit topic with her."

I frowned. "So she's never said anything to any of you?"

"Only that it's not something she wants to talk about," Chuck said. "At least not with us."

"Did you ask her?" Rob asked.

I nodded. "She doesn't want to talk about it," I confirmed. The conversation turned to the plans for Chuck and Terry's wedding, and I started cleaning up the dishes. I was only half listening, still focussed on my own unanswered questions, when I thought I heard my name.

I started paying more attention to the talk at the table and found that Terry was discussing the seating arrangements for the reception with Sandra, who apparently worked for a catering company. Sandra said, "So we'll put Brian with me and Michael's family. There's room for one or two more at that table, so if he brings a date, that'll be no problem."

"Um," I eloquently broke into the conversation. "Are you talking about me?"

"Yeah," Terry said. "Why? Is there a problem?"

"No problem," I said. "I guess I just wasn't expecting to be invited. I mean, we only met yesterday."

"True enough," Terry said, "but you have to come. You're family."

14
STEELY DO

I **WAS EIGHTEEN YEARS OLD,** still living with my parents and trying to navigate the hardest schoolwork I'd ever imagined. Looking back, it sounds like it should have been hell, but that year was one of the best of my life.

I'd thought that once I turned nineteen, it would be like something out of a fairy tale. My birthday would roll around, I'd register with the government agency and poof! There my real parents would be. Like magic. It never once occurred to me that it might not be that easy, that it might take a decade of searching. Back then I thought it was just a matter of a few months. It felt kind of like freedom.

It took Celia-Dee a while to make her move, but that didn't bother me. It's not like there was any chance I was going to be the one to take things to the next level, as they say. Even if I'd had the cojones to take the initiative, Seedy made it pretty clear who was in charge. She was the one who'd stolen my sandwich and she was the one who sought me out in the Engineering Building on campus. We'd been hanging out for a couple of weeks before I even found out that she was a Comp Lit major.

"What exactly is Comparative Literature?" I'd asked one afternoon over coffee.

"You remember all those horrible essay questions in high school English?" she asked in return. "You know: 'Compare and contrast the symbolism of birds in Margaret Laurence's *The Stone Angel* and Looney Tunes' Sylvester and Tweety.' Well, that's all we do in CL. Compare and contrast."

"Sounds like you don't like it much," I said, sipping my coffee.

"Eh," she shrugged. "It's okay." She stirred her tea. "But it's not that cool, either. I should have been an engineer," she said. "Too bad I got fifty-five percent in math."

I laughed. "That would be an impediment," I said, and she grinned.

We must have made a pretty funny-looking pair. I looked like the standard university dork — tan cords bought on sale from the Bay, a tee shirt with nothing cool on it whatsoever and a pair of grubby white runners. Utterly nondescript. Seedy, on the other hand, was a walking fashion bomb. That afternoon she wore a white shirt with tiny military airplanes all over it that she'd gotten from Value Village, with a pair of brown cargo pants with a bazillion pockets. She'd rolled the pants up to her knees and you could just see a mismatched pair of stripy socks peeking between the tops of her boots and the bottom of her pants. On the back of her chair hung her German army surplus jacket. In gold fabric paint she'd painted tiny anarchy symbols on the shoulders where the epaulettes would have been.

And then there was her hair. It was dark, nearly black, though she never dyed it to get that colour. She wore it short, its length varying from about fifty millimetres to ten centimetres. I never knew whether it was a totally nonchalant home haircut or a hundred-dollar salon job. Most of the time she just let it do whatever it wanted, but when she was dressed up for a gig she gobbed it up with gel and hairspray and who knows what until it stuck out all over like a porcupine and was as hard as a helmet.

At one of the Scream's shows, the bassist for the opening band became fascinated with Seedy's hair. It was a sweatbox in the club that night and everyone looked like a drowned rat after a couple of hours. Except Seedy. Not a single hair moved the whole night. After they were done playing, the bassist

— I want to remember his name as Ernest, but that's probably wrong — poked at Seedy's hair with his finger every chance he got. He was a bit of a mess. He'd been drinking a lot at the gig and he'd pre-loaded with something beforehand, but Seedy was in a generous mood. She'd let him poke at her hair for half an hour when finally he said, awestruck, "That's one steely do you got there."

The name stuck and many a night Seedy would let me know we were going out by saying, "I've got to get my steely do on." But that was still a ways off.

WE'D BEEN HANGING OUT FOR MONTHS; so long that I was convinced she just wanted to be friends. I, of course, was hopelessly in love with her. She was easily the coolest person I'd ever met. She made Angela Hoeffer look boring. She gave me a bunch of mix tapes with all these old bands — Black Flag, the Clash, Iggy and the Stooges, the Ramones. There was newer stuff in there, too — Nomeansno, the Dead Milkmen, NOFX. I'd never heard most of it before and it felt like a real education.

But she was more than just a punk rock girl who dressed like Minnie Pearl. She talked about books and movies like they were more than just stuff you consumed to escape real life. And she was fascinated by engineering. She made me tell her something new every day from one of my classes, and I even got her kind of understanding linear algebra. She was awesome. I'd finally convinced myself that I was lucky just to get to hang out with her, that I'd be perfectly happy worshipping her from afar, when she kissed me.

We were in my room, listening to a Johnny Cash album she'd just picked up. I was doing my homework and I thought she was doing hers. Maybe she was and she just got bored. Out of nowhere, she said, "Hey, BeeGee."

"Yeah," I looked up from my problems to find her nose almost touching mine.

"Do you like me, Brian Gumbo?"

"Of course I do," I stammered.

"I mean, *like me* like me?" she said, almost menacingly.

I gulped. My voice came out low. I hoped it sounded sexy, but it was probably just froggy. "Of course I do." Our mouths met in slow motion. It was easily the best kiss of my life, before or since.

WE NEVER REALLY TALKED ABOUT IT, but you could say we dated for a few months. It wound down over the summer, but for the last part of first year I was one happy guy.

Seedy didn't like labels. When my Dad figured out what was going on, and started badgering me to bring "my girlfriend" over to meet him and Mom, I honestly got to say, "She's not my girlfriend." That worked for only a couple of weeks; then he finally said, "Well, whatever she is, bring her over. We're not going to bite."

Of course not. It was Seedy who'd be doing the biting, I figured. Though as it turned out, Mom and Dad liked her well enough. She didn't try to be anyone other than herself with them, but she kept the F-bombs out of the conversation and seemed to be genuinely interested in both Mom and Dad. She and Mom had a long discussion about all-ages music shows and how to keep rowdy crowds from ruining everyone else's good time. While they solved that social problem, I helped Dad with the apple pie.

"Your not-girlfriend is something else," he said, grinning. I blushed and agreed. "Just be careful," he added more seriously.

"Dad," I said, getting redder in the face. "I've known about condoms since seventh grade. I get it, okay?"

He nodded, then said, "Good. That's not what I meant, though." He looked in toward the dining room, where Mom was laughing at something Seedy had said. "I mean she could break your heart. She's a strong personality, that one, and they are always the hardest to let go." I followed his eyes and saw him looking at Mom. He looked back at me. "Just remember that things change, Gumbo. But in the long run, it's usually worth it." He handed me two plates of apple pie with huge scoops of ice cream and shoved me back into the dining room.

GUYS LIKE TOM SPINDLE AND RYAN DEVINE didn't get me and Seedy. They called her things like *bad influence* and *distraction*. I don't know whether they were jealous or just thought I was punching above my weight. Maybe they really were concerned for my grade-point average. I never bothered to try to explain it to them; I just hung out with them less.

The truth was that when I was with Seedy, I was more than just another gearhead. Sure, she dug my nerdy nature, but she never felt like she couldn't talk about anything else. On any given day we'd argue about whether Batman was a real superhero (me: yes, because he's a larger than life hero plus, tights and cape! her: no, because he's just a normal man with money, gadgets and rage), whether Gabriel García Márquez was a romantic or not (me: no, because he depicts the reality of poverty; her: yes, because love is so palpable in his stories that it's almost a character in its own right) and whether you'd take the red pill or the blue pill (me: red, for learning the truth; her: red, for learning kung fu).

We told each other everything. She fantasized about being a mad scientist, inventing flying machines and doomsday devices, living with an army of robot servants. I wanted to be a surf bum on a beach in Hawaii. She had barely passed any of her science and math classes, and I'd never swum in the ocean. We could spend hours just imagining each other's future lives, complete with wardrobes, professional challenges and musical soundtracks.

We both lived with our parents, so sex was always a challenge. We did it in cars, in the woods, at other people's houses, behind the library and once in the library. I turned nineteen while we were together and, while she'd gotten me into a lot of her gigs when I was still eighteen, now I could be a real part of the entourage. I became the Technicolor Scream's primary roadie, in that I was the only roadie. I helped them set up their gear and drove the van when it was my turn to be the designated driver. I was always kind of amazed at how responsible the members of a rock band could be.

The summer after first year, the Scream broke up. Todd, the drummer, decided to move to Fort McMurray to work on the oil rigs. After he left, the band just broke down. They went through three drummers in as many weeks, then tried to play without a drummer at all. It didn't take long before they just gave up.

Todd was always the quietest of the four of them, and I was surprised that his departure made such a difference. After the final blowout (and it was a blowout: you've never seen people yell at each other until you've seen three slightly drunk members of a punk band yell at each other), Seedy was at my house, crying on the couch over the breakup. "Todd was the glue. He was the fucking glue that held us all together." I tried to put my arm around her, but she pushed me away with such force that I fell off the couch. After that I just sat there and waited for her to be done.

We only lasted a couple more weeks ourselves. I don't know exactly what drove us apart. At the time I blamed Todd and the breakup of the Technicolor Scream. Maybe that was part of it, but it was also just time. On my birthday I'd registered to find my birth parents and I was expecting them to walk through the door any day. Where Seedy and I used to talk about ideas, I talked about finding my roots and she brooded about the band. We'd both changed, but it hadn't happened together.

When we actually broke up, it was almost a relief. It was years later before I realized that it also felt like something important had died.

15
I WENT TO A GARDEN PARTY

THE WEEKS AFTER THE CAMPING TRIP to Maple Bay flew past in a daze. I barely had time to think about anything. The weekend after I'd gone up to Kim's house, I went to my parents' for the usual Sunday dinner. They were more curious about Kim and the rest of the family than I had ever expected. And, of course, they found the whole bit with the parrots fascinating.

"So, she just takes all the reject birds home?" my mom asked for the hundredth time. "How can she take care of them all?"

"Jeannette, that's her youngest daughter," I explained, "still lives at home and helps out. But I really got the impression that birds aren't that hard to take care of. If they live together, which they do, they amuse each other. And Kim supposedly has an amazing ability with birds."

"I think it's great that someone looks after the animals that aren't nicely domesticated little amusements for people," Dad said. He'd always been kind of put off by the idea of taking animals out of the wild, so there were never pets in our house. "Just because a bird doesn't want to play nice with the humans doesn't mean it has no right to live."

Mom and I shared a glance, hoping that Dad wasn't about to go on another tear about how people destroy nature or some such. She jumped in to change the subject, just in case. "And all the other kids," she said, "it sounds like they're a bunch of characters."

I nodded. "They are. Everyone is really nice, though, and I was amazed at how cool they all were with me being there. It's like they've been finding long-lost relatives their whole lives or something."

Now it was Mom and Dad's turn to share meaningful eye contact. I took a sip of my beer, and then Dad cleared his throat. "So, you'll never guess what we heard."

"Oh?"

"Carole McKirk called us the other day. She's going to be a grandma."

"Really?" I said. "Is Jacquie pregnant?" It still felt vaguely sickening to say that phrase, even all these years later.

"No," Dad said, shaking his head. "You remember Angela Hoeffer?"

"Sure," I said, confused.

"Well, it turns out that she and Blair McKirk have been living together for a few years now and they're going to have a baby in December."

"Whoa," I said. "Why would they want to do that?"

THE LAST I'D HEARD ABOUT ANGELA, she had taken a year off before university to go volunteer in some Latin American country planting trees or building hospitals or something. Blair had gone to UVic, same as me, but he did something in Arts — Poli Sci or Sociology; something interesting but pointless. I lost track of him long before graduation.

When I got back to my apartment, I called Johnny Frazier to see if he'd heard the news. He had no idea, so I filled him in on what Dad had said.

"I wonder how he pulled it off," Johnny said.

"What do you mean?" I asked, laughing. "You still don't know where babies come from?"

"Dumbass," he said. "I mean, how did he finally convince Ange to go out with him? He's been mooning over her since we were five years old and she never looked at him twice that way. I wonder what changed."

"Beats me," I said. "But you can't tell what women will do. They're like some kind of black-box system with alien programming in there. There's no rational method to decode it."

"Dude," Johnny said. "You know that's bullshit, right?"

"I calls 'em like I sees 'em," I said and hung up. I often wished I'd kept in better contact with Blair and Ange, and it felt particularly strange to hear about them from my parents. We had been so close once, the four of us, it was hard to imagine that we could ever be so isolated from each other that I didn't even know where they lived.

I supposed that I could call Carole McKirk and ask for their number. I'm sure she'd give it to me; she was always nice to us. But it felt like admitting to some kind of weakness of friendship to have to call Blair's mom to find him. I put it off.

INSTEAD I SPENT THE EVENINGS OF THE NEXT WEEK cataloguing my contacts. I'd kept every phone book — first paper, then electronic — I'd ever had, and spent the time making a spreadsheet with every person on the lists cross-referenced with all their old phone numbers, addresses and emails. I tried to date everything I could, but I was struck by how easily I'd lost track of so many people. I felt the stabbings of guilt common to all poor correspondents.

After the camping trip, I'd gotten a Facebook friend request from Jeannette and didn't know what to do. I wasn't a Facebooker before; it seemed kind of pointless. I already had my phone books — what did I need a special site to keep in touch with my friends for? But what about Jeannette and the others? We weren't friends — we hardly knew each other. But we weren't really family either, not in the sense that we're in each other's hair all the time like I was with Mom and Dad. I did know that I wanted some kind of contact with Jeannette and the others, but I didn't want to seem like a pest.

I guess this is also what the internet is for.

The next Sunday afternoon, Mom informed me that Carole McKirk was hosting some kind of neighbourhood party to announce and celebrate her upcoming grandmotherhood. I'd be invited along with Mom and Dad — apparently she was trying to outdo the Wilsons' daughter's engagement party from last year. Blair and Angela, the guests of honour, would be there, and it seemed like a good way to find out what was going on. I said I'd go.

"Any idea if she's invited the Fraziers?" I asked. Johnny's parents had moved from the neighbourhood a couple of years back, but I knew they still kept in touch with a lot of the folks. "I know Johnny will want to go."

"I don't know," Dad said, "but Carole is looking to inflate the guest list anyway. I'll put a bug in her ear the next time I see her."

Johnny called me the next night to tell me about the party at the McKirks'. "I heard," I said and passed on what my parents had said.

"Well, were you going to tell me?" he asked.

"Sure," I said. "I just wanted to make sure you guys were invited first."

"You're a tool," Johnny said, but I didn't understand why. He was like that sometimes.

"You're going, right?" I said. "It would be weird to be the only one there who didn't know what was going on."

"I doubt you would have been," Johnny said. "I think Blair and Ange dropped off the radar a long time ago. This is news to everyone."

CAROLE MCKIRK WAS ALWAYS AN OVERACHIEVER in the entertainment department. She always kept the best snacks, she let us watch TV in the afternoons and she threw awesome parties. But by the time we were in middle school, birthday parties had long passed being cool, so I forgot how great she was at organizing an afternoon yard party.

Johnny and I drove in together on Saturday afternoon, and I was immediately transported back in time to someone or another's sixth or seventh birthday party. There was the long rented table with bowls of chips, dips, cookies, chocolates and the pretty superfluous veggie sticks, along with two giant bowls of iced punch. Multicoloured streamers wound through the branches of the trees and along the awning over the deck. There was a whole block's worth of patio furniture: folding lawn chairs, side tables and even several round tables with umbrellas. Mrs. McKirk could easily have had a career as an events planner. I sometimes forgot that she was a stockbroker.

There had to be fifty people there already. I recognized a few faces — Mr. and Mrs. Frazier and Johnny's sister Mary, Mr. and Mrs. Hoeffer, some other people from the neighbourhood who looked familiar but I couldn't place. The rest of the people were strangers. It wasn't too surprising. Mrs. McKirk would have invited all her friends, and I wouldn't have known them twenty years ago, let alone now. Plus there had been the usual amount of turnover in the neighbourhood since I moved out and I hadn't kept up with the new arrivals.

Johnny went over to talk to his folks, and I hit up the food table. Laden down with a paper plate of goodies and a cup of punch, I stood by a small table under the shade of a big oak and nibbled and watched. I hadn't seen either Blair or Angela since I got here, but that didn't mean they weren't here. I wondered how they felt about all this hoopla. Judging by the median age of the crowd, it was obvious that this party was really for Mrs. McKirk, not them.

I was licking spinach and feta dip off my fingers when I felt a sharp poke in my ribs and heard a low voice say, "Hey, Gumbo. Welcome to the circus."

I turned and saw Angela half hiding behind me and the tree. She looked good. She had a little belly bulge that I wouldn't have even noticed if I weren't looking for it, but otherwise she was her usual wiry bundle of energy.

"Hi, Ange," I said. "It's good to see you. It must be, what ..." I counted mentally, "something like ten years now?"

"Yeah," she agreed. "Maybe more. I don't know if I saw you after I got back from Guatemala."

I shrugged. "Hard to say. So, what have you been doing?"

"Other than being the hapless fool lucky enough to make Carole McKirk's lifelong dream of becoming a granny come true?" she said, a trace of true meanness in her voice.

I decided to ignore that. "Yeah, other than that?" I grinned and she smiled too.

"Well, long story short," she said, "I worked for Oxfam after Guatemala, then Greenpeace and now I'm the western coordinator for Food Not Bombs."

"Cool," I said.

"Yeah," she said. "They say you get more conservative as you get older, but that's sure not the way it worked for me. Who knows where I'll end up next. Running some crypto-anarchist group that doesn't even have a name, probably."

I laughed. "Sounds about right," I said. "You should either spend a lot more time with Johnny or make sure you never see him again."

"How come?" she asked.

"He's a Crown prosecutor now," I said. She laughed. "So, how did you hook up with Blair again?"

"Again isn't really the right word," she said. "We always stayed friends, though we didn't hang out much in high school. After I got back from Guatemala, we hooked up. He's a social worker, so we found ourselves together at a lot of political gigs. He asked me out a few times, but I just wasn't seeing what was in front of me. I mean, we'd been friends forever, so it seemed weird to go on a date with basically your best buddy. But it turned out that he was right. We're pretty good together and we shacked up something like six or seven years ago. He'd know for sure."

"Wow," I said. "I never saw that coming. You always seemed so, I dunno, self-sufficient."

She laughed. "Yeah. I wasn't exactly the marrying type. But Blair is good for me, we're a good team. And regardless of his mom, I'm really looking forward to this." She rubbed her belly and smiled.

"Well, congratulations," I said. "To both of you."

"Thanks," she said. "And thanks for giving me a few minutes to hide out. It won't last forever. Carole's going to put me on display as soon as she sees me. But it was really good to talk to you again, Gum. We should try to keep it to less than a decade next time."

"Yeah," I said, fishing out my wallet for a business card. I wrote my cell number and email on the back and gave it to her. "Let's get together sometime — away from all this," I said, jerking my head back to the yard full of people.

"I'll call you," she said and kissed me lightly on the cheek. "But for now, duty calls." She squared her shoulders and marched into the fray.

16
CLEANING THE KITCHEN

IT ARRIVED THE WEEK AFTER CAROLE MCKIRK'S party. At first, I didn't know what it could be. The envelope was cream-coloured, heavy stock with a gold foil seal. It was the kind of thing I imagined the Nobel Prize would come in. It had my name in a fancy font on the front, or I would have thought that there had been a mix-up at the mailboxes.

Of course, it was the wedding invitation.

Teresa Jean Frost & Charlotte Hildegard Prokopnik
cordially invite you and a guest
to help celebrate their marriage
August 13, 2011, 4:00 P.M.

There was a stamped RSVP card included with the invitation. It had several options I could tick — Yes, I was attending; No, I wasn't attending; Yes, I was attending with a guest.

With a guest. I knew what that meant: a date.

Maybe it was a sign of the times — fewer people bothering to formalize their relationships, fewer people bothering to settle down at all. Maybe it was a sign of my lack of friends. Whatever the reason, this was the first wedding invitation I'd ever received. I'd been to a wedding before, some distant cousin of Mom's or something got married when I was a kid and we all went. But I was a kid, and kids get to run around under the tables and sneak sips of wine at weddings. Adults are expected to show up in a nice suit with a nice date. Even I knew that much.

Maybe I could bring Johnny. Surely a same-sex date would be acceptable at a gay wedding. Or would they be offended, since we're not actually a couple? And how do you ask that kind of question? Who knew that family would be so complicated?

I PUT THE INVITATION ASIDE FOR A DAY or two and spent my free time cleaning out my kitchen cupboards. To be honest, it was a little early for that. Kitchen clean-out wasn't on the schedule until late August, but I needed something to ease my mind, and scrubbing cupboards was a particular balm. I stacked my plates on my small kitchen table and set to work. Vacuum, soapy water, bleach, rinse, dry. The orderly steps calmed me and filled the hour between dinner and DVD time.

The phone rang while I was kneeling on the countertop and scrubbing the top shelf of the pantry. The obnoxious ringtone I was using that week startled me, and I wanged my head on the roof of the shelf. I slid off the counter, rubbing my sore head, and grabbed for my phone. The caller ID said Kim. I tried to compose myself.

"Hello?"

"Hi, Brian," she said. "It's Kim here. How are you doing?"

"Fine," I lied, my head throbbing. "And you?"

"Great," she said. "Busy as hell with all the wedding stuff, you know how it is." I made some positive noise and she went on. "That's why I'm calling. We're having a rehearsal next week-end and then the usual big family dinner after. I was hoping you'd come for the dinner. And I was also hoping you'd bring your parents. I'd really like to meet them, if that's all right with you. And with them, too, I guess." I couldn't get a word in. I wondered if she was actually nervous. It hadn't occurred to me that anything could faze her. "I know that some people would find it a bit awkward, so I don't want them to feel bad if they don't want to come. But please tell them that we'd all really like it if they could make it. With all the other people there, I'm hoping they'd feel less conspicuous, but we can do it some other time if they'd rather. It's just ..."

I finally just interrupted. "Kim," I said and she was quiet. "I'll ask them. I don't know what they'll say, but I'll ask, I promise. Email me the details of the dinner and I'll let you know what they say, okay?"

"Okay," she said, relief evident in her voice. "Thanks, Brian. Oh, and we're all looking forward to seeing you, too." She paused for a moment, and I thought I could hear the shuffling of paper. "I don't think we got your RSVP yet ..."

"Yeah," I said. "I'll send it soon ... I'm coming, I just ..." I took a breath. "I'm not, you know, seeing anyone and I, uh ..."

"Oh, don't worry about that," Kim said. "Just come on your own. You know enough people to get by without needing a date. I'll just mark you down as a yes. And if things change, don't worry about it. There's enough room for an extra person."

"Okay," I said, feeling embarrassment flush over me. This was just as bad as talking to Mom.

THE WAS A LOT OF NEWS TO PASS ON AT DINNER with the folks on Sunday. I'd somehow neglected to mention the wedding, which took about an hour to explain. "So, Chuck's a woman?" Mom asked after I thought we'd finally gotten through it all.

"Yes," I said, exasperated. "Short for Charlotte. You know, Charlotte, Charlie, Chuck. Her fiancée, Terry, is also a woman. They're getting married in a few weeks, and I'm going to the wedding. There's a big dinner next weekend after the rehearsal, and we're all invited. You, me and Dad. They want to meet you both."

"Those things are usually just for family," Dad said. "It seems weird to be invited to that."

"Yeah," I said. "They're pretty loose with the definition of family, I think." I looked at Dad and Mom and was surprised to see them both looking like they didn't know what to say. "Kim thought that being part of a big group would help — that you'd feel less like you're on show or something. She's happy to meet some other time if you'd rather."

This information didn't seem to ease their minds one bit. Finally, Mom said, "This is a lot to digest all at once, Brian. I mean, we always knew that it was possible you'd want to find your birth parents someday. And always, in the back of our minds, we knew that you'd probably meet them and that they might become a part of your life. But I don't think we ever thought ... I mean, I never thought that they would become part of *our* lives." She broke off and looked out the window.

Dad picked up where she left off. "It's not that we don't want to meet them, Gumbo," he said. "It's just that it's tough. We've spent all this time being a family, just the three of us; it's hard to deal with the fact that all of a sudden there's all these strangers ... It's just hard to know what to do."

"Well, it's up to you," I said. "You don't have to do anything you don't want to, and I'm sure no one is trying to make any kind of claim on you, or on me or anything. They're just curious, is all. Aren't you curious, too?"

They looked at each other. "I've only ever been grateful to the people who brought you into the world," Mom said, her eyes wet. "All I've ever thought about them was that I was so lucky that they were able to give us the child we wanted so much."

"I never wanted to know much about them," Dad said. "I wanted to get to know you myself, without any of the genetic or sociological baggage that knowing about your birth parents would pile on. So it's hard, after all these years of just kind of ignoring them, to all of a sudden be forced to recognize that these are real people, real human beings, you know?"

I nodded. "You don't need to decide now," I said. "Just let me know before the day so I can let them know whether to expect you or not." I knew I should leave it alone, but before I could stop myself I said, "But whether you like it or not, they are my family. It would be nice if you met them."

They both looked at me with pained expressions. Mom looked like I'd just slapped her and Dad had his *I'm very disappointed in you* face on.

"Family isn't about genetics, Brian," Dad said. "I would have thought you'd know that by now. I'm sure they're lovely people and I'm glad you're learning about your roots, but don't be fooled. They may be related to you by blood, but they don't know you and you don't know them. They are not ..."

"Dom," Mom said, stopping Dad from going on. "You're going to say something you regret. Brian." She turned to me. "You're going to have to give us a little time with this, okay?"

"Sure, Mom," I said, getting up. "I'll clean up." I picked up the stack of dishes and started to walk into the kitchen with them.

"No," she said, and I stopped. "I'll do it later. You should probably just go now. I'll call you later in the week, okay?"

I didn't know what to say. I left the dishes on the kitchen counter, said goodbye and drove back to my apartment. It was ten after seven, I was thirty years old and it was the first time I'd ever been kicked out of my parents' house.

17
MEET THE PARENTS

I **WAS KNEE DEEP IN A SPEC REPORT** for a new repair site on the Malahat when the phone rang. I was expecting Sandeep to call to discuss suppliers, so I just picked up without looking.

"Hi, Brian," Dad said. "Is this a good time?"

"Sure," I said, though really I was busy. "What's up?"

"I, uh," he said, "I'm sorry for some of the things I said the other day. I was just surprised, and ..."

"It's okay," I said. "I didn't mean what I said, either. Not the way it sounded, anyway." I kept my voice down. It was an open-plan office and I didn't really want to be having a big personal conversation where anyone could hear.

"Anyway, your mother and I have decided that we'll come to this dinner. It's not going to be easy, but it probably will be less horrible if there's a lot of other people who don't know each other there. We'll manage."

I smiled, but tried to keep too much happiness out of my voice. I could tell that they were doing it for me, not because they wanted to. "Thanks, Dad," I said. "I'll let them know. You want to drive out together?"

"Sure," he said, sounding a little less miserable. "That would be nice."

"Okay, I'll call you tonight to organize it."

"Thanks, Gumbo," he said. "I love you."

"I love you too, Dad," I said, and I almost didn't care who overheard it.

"YOU'RE SHITTING ME," JOHNNY SAID on the phone. "You are not seriously taking your mom and dad to the wedding rehearsal of the daughter of your birth mother. I can't even believe I just said that sentence. It's crazy."

"What's the problem?" I asked. "Kim and the rest of them want to meet my parents. Why shouldn't they?"

"You are such a moron," Johnny said. "Honestly, I only ever kind of understood why you'd want to meet your birth parents. I mean, on the face of it, it sounds like the kind of thing that makes sense, but when you really think about it, what's the point?"

"What do you mean, 'What's the point?'?" I asked, my voice getting louder. "This is my mother and father we're talking about here."

"No, Brian, it isn't," Johnny said in what I thought of as his *closing arguments* voice. "Shirley and Dom are your mother and father. They are the ones who changed your shitty diapers, who watched you take your first step, who took you to emergency that time you fell out of the tree."

"That was Angela's fault ..." I began, but Johnny cut me off.

"For Christ's sake, that's not what I'm talking about," he said. "I'm talking about who your parents, your *real parents,* are. Anyone can get knocked up, anyone can have a baby. That doesn't make you a parent. Being there, loving your kid, that's what being a parent is. And it seems to me like you're forgetting that right now."

"You wouldn't understand," I said.

"Probably not," he admitted. "But there's plenty you're not understanding, too, that's a lot more important. Think for a second about what it's like for them, for Shirley and Dom, while you're gadding about on this journey of discovery. How do you think this makes them feel, Gum? Maybe you need to spend a little time thinking about that." He hung up on me and I sat there with the dead phone in my hand for a long time.

I PICKED UP MOM AND DAD on the way to the Maple Bay Yacht Club where the dinner was being held. Dad folded himself into my small back seat and let Mom sit up front with me. They were both dressed up a little; Mom had even put on makeup. It wasn't until I saw the red lipstick that I really understood what Johnny was trying to tell me. They reminded me more of teenagers trying to make a good impression on someone's folks than grown people on a night out. I wondered if I'd made some terrible mistake.

It seemed like Kim had invited everyone she'd ever met to the dinner. There were more people there than I could possibly meet, and I recognized only a handful of them. When we first walked into the dining room, Mom's face took on that wary look all cops get when they're walking into a potentially dangerous unknown situation. Dad just looked like he was going to puke. In a few moments, though, they both calmed down. There was a kind of anonymity in the huge crowd that put us all at ease.

I was scanning the room for someone to introduce them to when I felt a hand on my shoulder. I turned to find Rob and Anna standing behind us. "Welcome to the madhouse," Rob said. "I don't know what Mom was thinking. This is going to be insane. I just feel bad for Terry."

"How come?" I asked.

"Because she's a sweetheart and doesn't deserve this kind of stress," he said. My parents had turned toward us now, hearing the sounds of a conversation.

"Rob, Anna," I said, gesturing for my folks to come closer, "these are my parents. Shirley Holmes and Dominic Guillemot. Mom, Dad, this is Kim's son Rob and his girlfriend, Anna."

"Very nice to meet you, Ms. Holmes, Mr. Guillemot," Anna said like a pro.

"Oh, please," Dad said, smiling. "Shirley and Dom are a lot less of a mouthful."

"Nice to meet you," Rob said. "It's probably going to be a bit of a gong show tonight, so if you need to hide out, the bar's that way." He pointed over his shoulder. "Well, I've got to go make the rounds. Good luck, you guys." He grinned and put his arm around Anna, who shot me a sympathetic look.

"They seem like nice kids," Mom said with a hint of surprise in her voice after Rob and Anna were out of earshot.

"They're all nice, Mom," I said. "Come on, let's go get this over with."

ON OUR WAY BACK FROM THE BAR, we ran into Chuck and Terry next. I got the impression they were trying to avoid the crowds, since we caught up with them in a corridor near the washrooms.

"Hey, look," Chuck said, catching my eye first. "It's Gumbo. Good to see you, buddy."

"Hi," I said, noticing Terry's eyes flitting to my parents. "Chuck, Terry, this is my mom and dad."

"I'm Shirley," Mom said, sticking her hand out to Terry, "and that's my husband, Dom. Congratulations to you both on your upcoming marriage." She beamed at them, and she and Terry shook hands. Mom turned to Chuck, who also shook hands quickly.

"I feel a bit like we're intruding on your celebration," Dad said with an apologetic smile. "There's an awful lot of people here."

"It seems to have developed a life of its own. If I'd known what we were getting into," Chuck said, "I might never had said yes when Terry proposed."

"Oh, shut up, you," Terry said, lightly punching Chuck on the arm. "We'd just have eloped, is all."

"Weddings can get kind of out of control," Mom said. "Ours was supposed to be just a small event, just family and close friends, and somehow we ended up with two hundred guests and a bill that we were still paying off five years later."

Dad reached over and put his arm around Mom. "But it was such a beautiful day," he said. "It was worth every penny." Mom shot Chuck a look that said *Maybe, maybe not*, and the two women shared a silent laugh.

A small, harried-looking man wearing an impeccable brown tweed three-piece suit came scurrying into the hallway. "There you are," he said to Chuck and Terry. "We need you with the wedding party for a few minutes before dinner."

"Duty calls," Chuck said with an exaggerated scowl. "It was nice meeting you. If we don't get a chance to talk later tonight, I hope we meet again in more reasonable circumstances."

"Thank you," Mom said and smiled warmly.

"I know it can be crazy right now," Dad said. "But you two try to enjoy it. You've got a whole lifetime to be quiet and content. For the next few weeks, you've got a licence to celebrate your love loudly. That's the point of this whole thing."

Terry smiled at him and patted his arm. "Thank you, Dom. That's great advice." She put an arm around Chuck and pulled her close, kissing her warmly. "Let's go, baby."

"You're such a sap," Mom said to Dad, her eyes twinkling.

"Someone's got to keep the love alive," he said, smacking her backside and making her giggle. My mother actually giggled.

"Dad," I said. "Knock it off."

"Okay," he said, grinning. "Let's go find some more people to meet." He took Mom's hand, and they walked into the dining room. I shook my head and followed.

DINNER GOT STARTED BEFORE I COULD FIND ANYONE ELSE I knew. As we all sat down, Kim stood with a slightly older couple who seemed to be as lost in the crowd as we were. "Good evening, everyone," Kim said, and the din quieted down. "I am so happy to be here with Alan and Gwen Frost, Terry's parents, as we celebrate the upcoming wedding of Charlotte and Terry." Polite applause and patient smiles from the happy couple. "There's a lot of people here, many of whom don't know each other. Weddings are such a wonderful excuse to get together with family and friends, and we're very lucky to have so many people here. Of course, there are some people missing as well, which is a shame."

I saw a dark look cross Chuck's face, and Rob and Jeannette shared a glance that might have been some cross between worry and embarrassment. I wondered what that was all about, but Kim went on without explanation. "But we have some additions as well to make up for it. I'd like to say a special hello to the Guillemots, who we're all hoping to get to know better over the next few years."

I felt my face get bright red as the whole table turned to look at us. Mom had her professional cop face on, her standard response to an uncomfortable situation, but Dad seemed to take the attention in stride. It must have been the two gin and tonics he'd had before dinner, because he confidently said, "We're so happy to be here and may I be the first to say congratulations to you and the Frosts on this wonderful occasion of your daughters' marriage."

The table broke into applause and a toast; I think everyone was happy to get back to the normal wedding speeches. After the toasting was done, Mr. Frost cleared his throat, cutting Kim off from any further speechifying. She looked a little put out, but was gracious enough not to take the floor back. He made some innocuous toast to some family member or another, and I tuned it all out. It was over soon enough, and the waiters brought out the salads.

For the next hour, we chatted with our table mates — Jeannette and a distant cousin of Terry's had somehow ended up in our area — and ate the institutional but reasonably tasty meal. Mom and Dad had polished off a bottle of wine between them, and Dad made a trip to the bar before dessert. It was a good thing I was driving, though I wasn't sure how the rest of the night was going to go. Dad returned with a pair of large cocktails for the two of them, just as I saw Kim make her way to our part of the room.

"Mr. and Mrs. Guillemot," she said, beaming at them.

"I'm Shirley Holmes," Mom said, not unkindly, "and this is my husband, Dom. You must be Kim."

Kim pulled a chair over and sat down at the table. "I'm so glad you agreed to come tonight," she said, glancing between Mom and Dad. "I realize that this is awkward —" she glanced at me, then back at them "— for all of us. But after meeting Brian, I wanted to meet you, too. He's such a fantastic young man that I wanted to meet the people responsible for that."

Mom looked a little confused, but Dad just grinned. "Thank you," he said. "We're proud of our kid."

"Rightfully so," Kim said. "You know," she said, scooting her chair a little closer, "I never doubted my decision. It wasn't easy, though, and every time I got pregnant after that I felt my heart break a little, wondering what had happened to my little man.

"But I knew that letting him go was the right thing to do; it was always the right thing to do. And when I finally met Brian, it was obvious that the people who had become his parents had done a great job. He's lucky to have gotten you two for parents." She turned to me. "You're very lucky."

Dad sniffed back a tear. He always got emotional when he drank gin. "We're the lucky ones, Kim," he said. "Thank you for giving us the best gift we could ever have received."

She smiled. "You're welcome, and thank you for being there. We all did well from each other, I think." She stood and laid a hand on Mom's shoulder. "I hope we see more of each other," she said, "but if it's not to be, I just want you to know how happy I am to have met you all." She smiled and turned to leave.

"Kim," Mom called after her, and she stopped and turned. "You have a wonderful family," Mom said, indicating the packed room. "Congratulations. We wish the best for your daughter's marriage."

"You're very kind," Kim said, smiling, and went back to the rest of the crowd.

WE LEFT SHORTLY AFTER THAT EXCHANGE, and the ride home was bizarre. Dad fell asleep in the back seat and Mom kept saying, "She's such a lovely woman, such lovely people ..." over and over again. I dropped them off and made sure they got inside before driving back home.

It had been an odd evening and I almost wondered why I'd gone. Obviously, Mom and Dad wouldn't have gone without me, but otherwise I seemed to be entirely superfluous. Still, Kim seemed happy, and even Mom and Dad appeared to be more comfortable about the whole thing than they'd been before. Of course, that could have just been the gin.

18
SEARCHING FOR THE GREENER GRASS

IT'S NOT THAT I FORGOT ABOUT the importance of my nineteenth birthday. Every day I expected to get the call, the letter that gave me a name. But it was a passive obsession. And being with Seedy — then the whole process of not being with her anymore — was kind of like being high. It was hard to access everything about normal life when there she was, occupying all my attention. And then brooding over the fact that she was gone.

It took about a year before I lost the hangover from the Seedy high, but by then nothing had happened on the parents front and I'd gotten wrapped up in schoolwork. There was the odd party, a girl or two, but nothing worth mentioning. All that changed when I graduated from university. I was done with waiting for things to happen.

I wanted to be out of school, finding my parents and starting my life. I wanted to get into the "real world," get a job, a car and my own apartment. The final year of school had been like pulling teeth. I could almost taste reality on the other side of exams, and it was sweet. Later, I wondered what the hell I'd been thinking.

I spent the entire summer after graduation looking for work. The campus job boards were a joke, but all the engineering jobs advertised in the paper wanted a P. Eng. or at least a few years' experience. It was a rough time, but it took my mind off the fact that the process of finding my real parents had totally stalled.

I'd registered with the provincial Adoption Reunion Registry on my nineteenth birthday, but since I didn't have the two hundred and fifty bucks to have them do a search for me, I was on my own. I might have been able to borrow the money from my parents, but I still didn't want to have that conversation with them. I'm sure they knew I was looking, but it felt like something that ought to be a secret. I didn't want them to think I was looking for something better. Even though that's kind of what I was doing.

Failing to find work was a perfectly good way to take my mind off it. I spent an hour a day with the Careers section of the newspaper, and I'd sent my resumé off to a half dozen placement agencies. By the time August rolled around, I was seriously starting to consider those construction jobs I'd looked into during The Thing with Jacquie. Either that or taking a college course as a paralegal. There seemed to be a million job ads for legal assistants.

Mom and Dad pretty much left me alone with my misery. Mom had just been promoted from Uniform Division to Detective Division; it was a big deal for her. It wasn't really more work, but she was trying to make a good impression, so she was pretty busy. Dad was Dad. He was working regular shifts at one of the high-rent seniors' places, plus subbing at the hospital in emergencies. He was still around more than Mom was, but it seems like I hardly saw either of them that summer.

I was moping around one afternoon, surfing the internet for adoption reunion sites, when I got a call from some woman named Emily Hunter. She told me she was a recruiter at Gill-Sanders. After a minute of confusion, I guessed that it was one of the placement agencies I'd contacted. I put on my best job-applicant voice and waited to see what she wanted.

"We received your cv, Mr. Gwee-mott," she mispronounced and I didn't correct her.

"Yes?" I prompted.

"And I'm afraid that it is very difficult to place a recent engineering graduate in the current economic climate."

"I see," I said, trying to keep defeat out of my voice.

"I don't think that we are going to be able to assist you with your employment search," she continued.

"Oh," I said, not knowing what to say. Why was she calling if they were just going to bin my resumé?

"However," she went on, and I felt my heart rate spike, "I have a few tips that may help."

"I'd be happy for any help," I said.

"Try the government job listings," she said. "The city, province and feds all employ a lot of people in the CRD and regularly have entry-level positions available. They all post their employment opportunities on the internet, and sometimes they're posted for only twenty-four hours. I'd recommend that you look daily."

"Thanks," I said, already bringing up Google to search for the job pages.

"It's no problem," she said, a smile in her voice. "I know how hard it is to find a job after graduation." She paused a moment, then said softly, "I spent a year after university working at a bookstore. I just got this job two months ago."

"I appreciate the help, Ms. Hunter," I said, "really."

"Good luck, Brian," she said and hung up.

I TOOK HER ADVICE AND THEN SOME. I was on the various job listings probably three or four times a day, even weekends. In four months, I applied to maybe twenty jobs and took exams and had interviews for a couple of them. It was getting to be Christmas time and I had convinced myself that it was never going to happen when I got the call for a job I'd applied for back in September. I'd completely forgotten about it.

I don't know what it was that cinched it, but I started my first day of my first job as an engineer just after the Christmas holiday. January 10. It wasn't much of a job, really. Mostly I was the assistant to a bunch of P. Engs who made me do all the boring work. Still, I was thrilled to be getting a paycheque for what I'd spent four years spending my parents' money to learn to do.

I spent my first cheque on taking Mom and Dad for a really nice dinner. I spent my second cheque on the fee for an adoption search. It took ten more cheques before I found myself a cheap apartment in the city and moved out of my parents' house. I was almost twenty-three years old.

MY APARTMENT WAS IN A PART OF TOWN they called Handgun Heights, which is hilarious in so many ways. First of all, we're talking about Victoria here. It's not exactly East L.A. The most dangerous thing in this town is the thousands of blind or dotty senior citizens who refuse to give up their drivers' licences.

Second, it's an example of how out of touch with reality people in this town are. My neighbourhood was cheap. Most of the places there were rentals, the houses cut into flats and the other buildings three- or four-storey walk-ups. All kinds of people lived there — students, folks who worked construction, shop owners, waitresses, artists, the odd drug dealer and the odd lawyer. Lots of people want or need inexpensive housing. But people in Victoria thought that cheap equalled dangerous, as if only criminals would live in anywhere less than a quarter-million-dollar place. It was bizarre.

The guy I worked with most closely at the City, a new P. Eng. named Jakob Ingel, was the worst. He was actually a really nice guy, but he'd lived in ritzy Oak Bay his whole life and was literally terrified of my perfectly nice neighbourhood. Once I'd been working with him a few months, and we'd gotten to know each other a little, he found out where I lived. He spent the next three weeks trying to convince me to move somewhere "decent."

"But I like it in the 'hood," I'd said, making phony gang symbols with my fingers.

"I know you make enough to afford somewhere better," Ingel said. He knew I was an Engineer Level One and the salary ranges for all City positions were public information. Plus, he'd started as a One himself a few years back.

"Sure," I conceded, "but why should I pay more than I have to? I like my apartment. I like my neighbours. There's an all-night diner a block away and I can walk to the grocery store. Besides, I'm saving for a car." I put on a fake menacing expression. "Plus all my homies be keepin' it real down the 'hood." I did a terrible fake gangsta accent and I don't think he got the joke.

"I don't get you, Gumbo," he said, then started talking about the plans for the new water mains in Langford.

I WASN'T ENTIRELY HONEST WITH JAKOB INGEL. I did like my neighbourhood just fine, but it wasn't like I was hanging out with my neighbours every night having burgers and beers on the front lawn. I didn't even know the names of anyone in my building. But I had other reasons for wanting to live somewhere cheap. Sure, I really was saving up for a car, but in the back of my mind I had this idea that when I found my parents I might need to travel to meet them.

I had a whole set of fantasies about them, new ones that seemed more realistic than the rock star and high-profile politician dreams of my youth. I guessed that they had been teenagers when I came along. So now, twenty-odd years later, they would be proper adults, with real jobs and lives. Maybe interesting ones, maybe not. But there was no reason to assume that they lived on the Island. In fact, the more time went by without any sign of making contact, the more likely it seemed that they'd moved away.

So I was squirrelling away cash like a miser, on the off chance that I might need plane tickets to somewhere expensive and exotic. Maybe my mom was an English teacher in Japan.

Maybe my dad was a chef in Paris. Who knew? I had to be prepared.

I STARTED MY NEW JOB along with three other people, all of us recent graduates. I knew all of them slightly — the lone woman in the group, Susan Somethingunpronounceable, I'd taken out once on a doomed date in third year. Thankfully, she seemed to have forgotten all about it by orientation.

It seemed like from the very first day on the job, the more senior people were telling the new hires how to get a new and different job. In training, we spent an entire morning on how to access the internal job listings and how to move up from level one to level whatever. They even told us about how to apply for jobs with the province and the federal government. If I hadn't known better, I'd have thought they were trying to get rid of us.

It was just part of the culture, though. Government jobs are strange like that. Pretty much everyone starts as a level one or two and works their way up the ranks by winning "competitions" for new jobs. Apparently the director of the department started as a mail room clerk. So, everyone has moving up as the number-one goal, and they want to get you on that treadmill as soon as possible. It's like moving up is what you're there to do, and the work is just what happens between competitions.

As much as it seemed strange to begin with, it didn't take long before I wanted to move up, too. Getting over the thrill of actually having a job in my field combined with the boredom of doing the same menial tasks day in and day out — plus the desire for a bigger paycheque — fuelled my entree into the Competition Club.

19
RESPONSIBILITY

THERE WAS A GROUP OF ABOUT TEN OF US who seemed to meet at every exam for the internal jobs. A couple of the guys I'd been hired on with would be there, plus a bunch of people who'd joined the department in the previous round of hiring. Even though the processes were called competitions, there was no competitive spirit among our group. We all talked about the questions after each exam, and when someone was called for an interview, we genuinely wished him or her well, even when we hadn't been lucky enough to get the call. It wasn't personal. It was just business. The business of moving up.

Out of all the competitions I was involved with, I placed a few times on the list, but I was never higher than third. Someone in third was so unlikely to actually get offered a position that you might as well not have made the list. Almost all the competitions were to fill a single vacancy, and while once in a blue moon the first-place candidate would refuse the job, it was nigh on impossible for both number one and number two to defer. Even so, third was worthy of congratulation, and it felt like a real accomplishment to see my name so near the top of that list.

The reality of the situation was that the Competition Club was hardly about getting a new job. It was what we did at work — which was sanctioned, even encouraged by our bosses — to avoid actually doing what we were hired to do. There's this myth that government workers are lazy or incompetent, but from what I've seen that's rarely the case. It's just that so much effort and energy is directed at tasks that have nothing to do with our actual jobs.

Aside from the Competition Club, there are the various charitable campaigns that department heads sign up for, all of which require committees of employees to run, all on work time. And there are innumerable meetings, all of which are ostensibly to further the stated purpose of the department, but which serve mainly to kill an hour of two of a workday and possibly even stymie a program of real work. It could have been maddeningly frustrating.

But after a few months, being at the bottom rung of that ladder had gotten boring, so I was happy enough to get out of doing real work. I'd rather be actually engineering something than heading up the annual blood drive, though, so moving up was my main priority.

IT WAS ONLY EVER A MATTER OF TIME. After eight months as a level one, I placed first on the list for a level three in the road maintenance department. It was finally a chance for something better than the mathematical equivalent of getting the coffee. The position even came with a tiny bit of control over the projects. I'd been careful in my interview to stress my desire for additional responsibility at work. It was the buzzword of the day, and all of us in the Club were using it liberally in our applications and interviews.

As it turned out, the "control" over the project was more like being the person management yelled at when things went sideways. All the real decision-making was delegated to a committee I didn't even sit on. Still, it was better than being a level one. And, of course, there was Audrey.

Audrey Michaels sat three cubicles down from me on the way to the printer. She was a financial clerk, a pay grade above me, but I guessed that was just because she'd started before me. She'd been with the department since she was in second-year university, as a summer intern. It was enough to get her foot in the door, so that when she graduated she was in full swing with the Club. She moved up fast.

She was about my age and seemed to be the most interesting person on our floor. On Monday mornings I noticed she sometimes had the telltale black mark of a bar stamp on the back of her hand or the inside of her wrist. She dressed pretty much like everyone else, the "business casual" that made the shareholders of the Gap rich, but there was something about her. Like she didn't take it all seriously, or that there was some great artistic spark hiding behind her ledgers and spreadsheets.

I started following her around after three weeks.

I WASN'T A VERY GOOD STALKER. I'm pretty sure she made me on day two at the Mongolian Wok in the mall; then she totally caught my eye at Munro's bookstore on day four. The day after she managed to sneak up behind me in the line at the Starbucks on the ground floor of our building when I went down for afternoon coffee.

"Funny to see you here," she said, smiling at me when I jumped at her tap on my shoulder.

"Uh," I stammered. "Hi, ah, Audrey."

She gave me a hard look, but I could see the corners of her lips being tugged up, as if by some invisible thread. "You've been following me," she said.

"Uh," I repeated, looking around for some means of escape. I seriously considered just bolting for the door, but that would only postpone the inevitable until I got back to my desk.

"Uh," I said again, then grinned in what I hoped was a disarming way. "Just trying to figure out what to do with myself on breaks." I shrugged. "Times like this I wish I smoked."

"What?" she asked, confusion on her face.

"The smokers all have a built-in set of buddies," I explained, "and places to go and things to do at coffee and lunch. As for me," I shrugged again, "there's only so much internet surfing at my desk I can stand."

She frowned as we reached the front of the line and I ordered my Friday treat of a Venti non-fat three-pump vanilla latte. "So, you're saying you were following me because you were bored?"

"Sort of," I said and moved aside so she could order.

"Can I have the tiny drip coffee that's not on the menu? Thanks," she said to the barista and turned to me without waiting for a response. "Huh," she said to me, the smile twitching at the corners of her mouth again. "And I here I thought you wanted to ask me out. Such a shame when I have tickets to Nomeansno this weekend and no date."

She turned away from me to collect her change and walked toward the counter to wait for her coffee.

A lot of questions were going through my brain all at once. Was she asking me out? Did this mean I was off the hook for the creepy behaviour? Starbucks has sizes of coffee that aren't on the menu? I asked the one that, oddly, screamed the loudest for attention. "How did you know I liked Nomeansno?"

"You're not the only one with observational skills," she said. "I saw the CD case for *Why Do They Call Me Mr. Happy?* on your desk the other day."

I took my latte from the counter and sipped. "So," I ventured. "You're looking to offload that extra ticket?"

"Nope," she said, stirring milk into her coffee. "But I am looking for a date." She looked at me over the top of her itty-bitty Starbucks cup as she took a sip. "Wanna go?"

OFFICE ROMANCES ARE A BAD IDEA. I didn't need to have one to know that. Luckily, Audrey moved to a different department on another floor about a month after we started dating, a promotion she knew was coming when she asked me out. She knew about office relationships, too.

She liked punk rock and wasn't shy about taking charge of our relationship. Even I could tell that it looked like I was just seeking a replacement for Seedy. Maybe it was something like that in the beginning, but being with Audrey was a lot more ... I don't know how else to put it than *grown-up* ... than being with Seedy had ever been.

I kept a toothbrush and a change of clothes at her apartment. We went grocery shopping together and cooked dinner for each other. We argued about money. I'm not sure there's anything that says "real relationship" more than arguing about money. And after we'd been together a year, it happened. We had The Fight. The fight I've had with every woman (except Seedy) that I've dated longer than a few months. The fight that always ends up in a break-up. All because of responsibility.

UNTIL THE FIGHT, THOUGH, things with Audrey were pretty great. I took her out to meet Mom and Dad one weekend in the summer. Dad was barbecuing hot dogs and burgers, and Mom had a night off for a change. We arrived at two in the afternoon and Dad immediately handed us a pair of cold beers. "Stay the night," he said, jerking his head toward the house. "I finally got around to setting up your old room as a guest room, but we never have any guests. You two might as well make use of it."

Audrey and I shared a glance at each other; then she smiled and took the proffered beer. "Thanks, Mr. Guillemot," she said. "We'd love to stay over."

"Excellent," Dad said, "and for heaven's sake, call me Dom." He turned toward Mom, who was coming into the yard with a tray of some kind of hors d'oeuvres. I couldn't remember ever having hors d'oeuvres at home. "And that's Shirley," Dad said. "Don't let her make you call her Detective, either. She's got to be off duty once in a while."

We talked all afternoon. Mom and Dad graciously pretended to be interested in municipal accounting practices while I just watched Audrey. It all seemed so easy for her — talking with them like they were just normal people, not her boyfriend's parents, for god's sake! And we were going to share a bed in their house. It all seemed like too much too fast.

I ate two burgers and three hot dogs and polished off the last of the baked pastries Mom had brought out in the afternoon. "He's still a good eater," Dad said to Audrey while I picked at something in filo pastry.

"He just eats when he's nervous," she said and patted my knee. I wanted to die.

MOM AND DAD LOVED AUDREY, of course, and I did, too. We'd settled into a happy rut, spending the weekends together, walking in to work together Monday morning. It wasn't hard to imagine a future where every day would be like Monday morning. I knew I ought to have felt like I was too young to be settling down so fast, like I should have more wild oats to sow. But Audrey was fun, she was good for me and I loved her. Why shouldn't we move in together? Someday.

20
TOO MUCH INFORMATION

You've been tagged in a post by Jeannette Andrews

I clicked on the link and was surprised to see a huge block of text. My name was highlighted in blue, but it had company. I recognized Rob, Anna, Chuck and Terry, but there were about a half dozen more names that didn't ring a bell.

"WARNING," the post began. All caps — I rolled my eyes. Whenever I met her, Jeannette seemed like a perfectly rational, sane teenager. But for some reason, on Facebook she was what Johnny would call a drama queen. I never really understood what he meant by that until I started reading Jeannette's Facebook posts.

> WARNING: grandma and grandpa Heinz are on fb and are making nasty posts on ppls walls. If you don't want there holy roller bs on yr page, CHANGE YOUR PRIVACY SETTINGS to friends only or block them. DO NOT ACCEPT THERE FRIEND REQUESTS!!! There only on here to make awful comments to ppl. Don't forget what they said to Terry.

This must be Kim's parents, I thought. I certainly hadn't had a friend request from either of them, but why would I? As far as I knew, they didn't even know who I was. Though this post might change all that.

I clicked over to Terry's wall and scanned down the posts. Most were wedding related, interspersed with a few links to library or book topics. I didn't see anything that looked like vitriol from Kim's parents.

I clicked over to Chuck's page and was scanning for anything juicy when I stopped myself. What was I doing, exactly? Poking my nose into the business of these people I really only barely knew. Certainly, Jeannette had drawn my attention to whatever it was that was going on, so she at least thought it related to me somehow. But really it didn't.

Still, I couldn't help but be curious. I'd noticed that Kim's parents were absent at the events I'd attended, though she'd made it clear that they still lived on the Island. I could imagine that they didn't approve of Chuck and Terry's wedding, but it felt like they were conspicuous in their absence. Like Rob's father, they were a presence by not being talked about.

I decided that surfing through my relatives' Facebook pages looking for gossip was normal, not creepy. Or maybe both, but I could live with that. I finished skimming over Chuck's wall, then clicked over to Rob's page. It didn't take long before I saw the comment to a years-old post about Rob and Anna moving in together.

> **Josef and Hannah Heinz:** Repent now, sinners, in the hour of your shame. The hour of your redemption is upon you — feel the light of our Lord in your heart and be saved.

If I didn't know better, I would have just thought it was spam. Rob had completely ignored it, as far as I could tell, though it was just as likely that he hadn't seen it. Jeannette obviously had, though, as she'd posted her own comment.

> **Jeannette Andrews:** Stop this! No one wants to hear your hurtful propaganda. Doesn't the bible say to love your neighbour as yourself? Shouldn't you at least try to love your own family as much?

I could tell from the timestamps that Jeannette had made her WARNING post right after that comment. I had to wonder what the point was. From what I could see, it was Rob's problem, not hers. And by drawing everyone's attention to their comments, she ensured more people saw them than if she'd said nothing. I didn't get it. It had nothing to do with her, and her post only made things worse from what I could tell.

Maybe it was a generational thing?

"SO, I DON'T KNOW WHAT TO MAKE OF IT, Gumbo," Johnny said. He took a bite of his omelette, leaving a smudge of Floyd's famous pesto hollandaise on his chin. He chewed and looked at me expectantly.

"I am the last person to ask," I said. "No one has ever sent me flowers, not at work, not three days in a row, not ever. I guess you've got an admirer?" I posited. Inside I was thinking how unfair it was that Johnny's major problem in life was who was sending elaborate bouquets to his office.

"Could it be a bribe?" I suggested, mainly because I didn't want to think about romance. I'd been alone so long at that point I'd just about given up.

His face took on a thoughtful look. "I guess it's possible," he said, "but there's no card and I don't know who would think that a bunch of daffodils would make any prosecutor throw a case. I mean, really." He lifted a forkful of hash browns to his mouth. Man, could Johnny ever eat.

"Anyway," I said, working to change the conversation, "I have to tell you about this thing I saw on Facebook." I gave him a brief synopsis of Jeannette's freak-out about her grandparents and waited for Johnny to finish his bite of food.

"Jesus," he said, missing the irony, "they sound like a pair of nutjobs."

"Sure," I said, "but what was Jeannette thinking? I mean, it's totally none of her business."

"Yeah, but she's just trying to protect you all. She's the youngest, right?" I nodded. "She probably thinks she's the only one who knows how the internet works. It's kind of sweet, really."

"I think it's weird." We spent a few moments in silent eating. Then I said, "Actually, what's weird is that the vast majority of what I know about the Heinz family is from stalking them on Facebook. I'm such a creep."

Johnny laughed. "You're not a creep," he said. "At least, no more than anyone else. If you can see it, it's meant to be seen. That's the whole point of stuff like that."

"I guess," I said. "And it's not all of them, at least. I hardly know Wolf's daughter June at all, because she's not on." I shook my head. "It never used to be this way. Jeez, I feel like such an old man: 'Kids these days don't know what life was like before the internet.'" I waited for Johnny's laugh, but it never came. Instead I saw he had his *deep thoughts* face on.

"What's wrong?" I asked.

"Biomom's last name is Heinz, right?"

"Yeah, that's Kim's name," I answered, a little pissed at his dismissal.

"And she's got a brother named Wolf?"

"Yeah."

"Short for Wolfgang?"

"I guess."

"Tall, silver fox, drinks dark beer?"

I frowned. "Yeah," I said. "You know him?"

Johnny laughed and slapped the table. "Hell, yeah," he said. "Wolf's my boss."

"God," I said. "Small world."

"Naw," Johnny said, "it's just a small town. We always forget that. How funny."

"I knew Wolf was a big-shot lawyer," I said, "but I never learned exactly what he does. So, he's your boss?"

"Think of it like this," Johnny said. "Imagine it's *Law and Order*, okay? He's Sam Waterston and I'm Jill Hennessy."

"Oh," I said, understanding completely. Part of me hated that Johnny patronized me like this, but it worked. It always worked.

"So, what does Wolf think about the great floral bouquet mystery?" I asked.

Johnny shrugged. "He knows I'm a player," he said without a trace of self-consciousness. "Probably hasn't even noticed."

"Eww," I said and did nothing when Johnny stole my last piece of toast.

21
THE FIGHT

AUDREY WAS NOT ONE OF THOSE NEUROTIC, paranoid
girlfriends that bad movies and early twenties male-
bonding conversations are filled with. If either of us
worried about the other one cheating, it was me. I didn't think
she was or anything, but I knew I wasn't going to be sneaking off
to hot sheet motels on my lunch hour, and Audrey knew it, too.
I was completely happy with Audrey. I could imagine a universe
where she wasn't as perfectly content with me, but I couldn't
imagine one where I wasn't. So if anyone was paranoid, it was me.

Except Audrey was weird about condoms. Not the whole
time, of course. Like every other woman I've slept with, she
insisted on condoms at the beginning as much as I did. It's not
like sex is exactly a safe activity in this day and age, my main
concern — pregnancy — notwithstanding. Condoms were the
solution, not the problem.

But once I'd been exclusive with a woman for several
months, the condom conversation started to morph in strange
and bizarre ways. As if *We've been together for X number of months*
is a valid reason to stop using condoms. Like, all of a sudden,
after so many months of exclusivity, all that perfectly good safe
sex is somehow inadequate. Like, after so many months of dating, there's no longer anything to fear.

Of course, they all say they are on the pill. And I'm sure
they are — I'm not accusing any of my ex-girlfriends of actually

trying to get knocked up. But there's no way I can be sure, not one hundred percent certain, that they are taking their pills regularly enough, or that they never forget, or even that they are taking them at all. There's no way, other than administering the tablets myself on a set schedule, that I can be sure. And I need to be sure. So, I don't have sex without condoms. Ever.

And, for some reason, my girlfriends all ended up hating that.

SEEDY AND I DIDN'T DATE LONG ENOUGH for it to come up, so it happened first with Audrey. It started slowly. Not knowing what was coming, I didn't see the signs. After about six months of dating, she announced that she was on the pill. I thought she was just telling me stuff about her life and I said something useless like, "Good for you," or "How much does that cost?" I forgot all about it.

A few times after that, we'd be in bed and I'd reach for the nightstand drawer. She'd say something like, "Do you have to?" and I'd laugh and say something like, "Why risk it?" or "No glove, no love." Eventually she tried the now-familiar line, "I want to feel you. Really feel *you* inside me."

That line has absolutely zero effect on me now, but the first time, when Audrey said it, her voice all husky with lust, I nearly fell for it. My hand actually paused on the way to the drawer and I briefly thought, "She's on the pill. We're both healthy. What's the worst that could happen?" Then I remembered The Thing with Jacquie and had a flash of what my life would become if Audrey got pregnant.

We both had good jobs, with excellent parental leave benefits, so the financial hardship I imagined back when I was eighteen was gone. But I still had the same constriction in my chest, the rising panic that the thought of unwillingly becoming a father had stirred in me six years previously. I still felt getting someone pregnant was the same life-ruining experience it would have been as a teenager.

I barely had my own apartment. I still didn't even own a car. I was technically an adult, but I was just a juvenile-adult. I could walk into a meeting at work and talk about steel torsion strength and million-dollar budgets, but I still felt like I needed a permission slip to walk onto a used car lot. I still felt weird every month when I paid my bills, like I was just practising at being a grown-up. I couldn't be a parent! It would be the worst thing that could happen to me.

It was a momentary flash, over in under a second. Probably Audrey wouldn't even have noticed if it hadn't immediately killed all desire in me. Her hand just happened to be in the perfect position to notice my physical and emotional deflation. I rolled away from her to avoid the look of confusion and hurt in her eyes. "I'm sorry," I mumbled into my pillow, not exactly sure what I was apologizing for.

"I don't get it," she said, holding me from behind and rubbing my back. "Most guys can't wait to get past the condom stage."

"I'm not most guys," I said, hurt and anger in my voice.

"I know, baby," she said, "and that's why I love you. It's just kind of odd, that's all."

"Yeah, well, I like to be safe," I said, still a hint of indignation left though I was starting to feel mollified. "Don't you want to be careful? I don't know what I'd do if you got pregnant," I said, softly.

"Okay," she said, and I thought that was the end of it. Foolishly.

SHE NEVER TRIED THAT LINE WITH ME AGAIN. Instead, she left it alone for a while, long enough for me to assume that everything was back to normal, that everything was okay. Then, out of what seemed like nowhere, she accused me of sleeping with someone else.

We hadn't even been fighting. We were at her place, putting the groceries away, and she happened to end up with a bag of non-food stuff. There was a box of tissues, some hand cream, shampoo and a box of condoms. I didn't know what was in the bag when she went crazy, so it was some time before I figured out what was really going on.

"You're fucking someone else, aren't you?" she said, wheeling around in the small galley kitchen. We were maybe two feet apart. It was unnerving.

"What?"

"That's the only explanation," she said, her voice rising dangerously. "You're fucking someone else."

"I don't know what you're talking about."

"You can't even deny it," she said, getting close to a shout. I was backing up, trying to put some space between us. I had no idea what was going on.

"I don't know what made you think this," I said, "but I'm not sleeping with anyone else. I love you, Audrey. I don't want anyone else."

"I don't believe you," she said, her voice back down to a more normal level. I knew I was really in trouble now.

"What made you think this?" I asked, hoping for some clue to the bizarre misunderstanding she must have had. "Is it all the time I've been spending online?" I guessed blindly. "I told you, I'm trying to find my birth parents. It takes a long time. You want to look at my email? You want proof?" I could hear the desperation in my voice.

She shook her head, and I thought I saw tears forming in her eyes. She wasn't much of a weeper, so I started to get scared. She really believed that I was cheating on her! How was this even possible? I'd never done anything ...

That was when she threw the box of condoms at my head. It caught me just above the eye and stung a surprising amount. I reflexively began to rub the spot, as Audrey recited, calm and mean, "Having multiple sexual partners is a risky sexual practice. You should use condoms every time you have sex to reduce the risk to you and your partners." She emphasized the *S* at the end of the last word and then shrieked, "Get out of my house!"

I fled.

WE TALKED A FEW TIMES AFTER THAT. She apologized and I apologized, but it was over. She didn't trust me and neither of us wanted to be in a relationship without trust, and that was all there was. When I went over to my parents' for dinner and told them we broke up, I said it just didn't work out. "It was a mutual thing," I said. It was technically true, but it didn't tell them anything of the real story. How could I explain to my parents that my girlfriend was so insecure about herself and so untrusting as to assume that I'd lie about something as important as birth control?

I was a wreck for a long time after Audrey and I split up. I had really loved her. I had started looking for apartments we might move into together. I thought she might be The One. But it turned out that she must have been hiding it for a year. The jealousy. I'd never told her about The Thing with Jacquie, or what I thought it must have been like for my real parents when I came along, but surely that was obvious. Assuming I was hiding something — that I was hiding an affair, of all things — I couldn't understand that.

I didn't want to be with a woman who thought all men were cheating, selfish bastards. I didn't want to be with a woman who could think those things and pretend that we were equals. For a long time, I didn't want to be with a woman at all.

I've had a half dozen girlfriends since Audrey and about half of those were serious enough to get to The Fight stage. At only thirty years old, I felt like I was really too young to be so cynical, but the truth is that I almost always had a sense of relief when it finally came to the end. It's like the monster hiding just out of sight in the shadows has finally shown itself, and now that you can see that it's just yesterday's shirt and a twisted-up coat hanger, you can finally stop being afraid and just get it over with.

Unfortunately, it inevitably means getting over the relationship, too.

22
THE RAINBOW ROOM

*O*BVIOUSLY, IT WOULD HAVE BEEN EASIER FOR ME if I'd been gay.
So, after one particularly nasty breakup, I tried. Kind of.

The idea came to me when in the dairy aisle. It was
Tuesday — grocery day. I stopped off at Thrifty's on my way
home from work, as I did each week. I was standing in front
of the yogourt, trying to decide whether it was a raspberry or a
blueberry week, when I noticed them. They were about my age,
much better dressed than I was, but otherwise similar enough.
They were obviously a couple, discussing the meal plan for the
week. The tall guy was checking items off a list written on the
back of an envelope while his boyfriend inspected the cheeses.
They looked so normal. It was what I had always wanted.

I thought about them the whole way home. Why couldn't
I have a relationship that was as easy as that? It was the part I'd
loved best with Audrey — simple domesticity. Dividing up the
household chores, cooking for each other. I'd never had that
feeling since, the simple happiness of being with someone you
love on a daily basis. The spectre of The Fight always took the
sweetness out of it.

Obviously, I didn't immediately think the solution was to
become gay. But as the weeks went on, I found that I couldn't
stop thinking about Ryan and Jim. At some point I'd given the
dairy-case guys names, jobs and hobbies in the fantasy life I'd
imagined for them. I pictured their apartment, immaculately

decorated in soft cream and teal. Ryan was a doctor, Jim an architect. They had a Labrador puppy, a massive DVD collection and a well-used Xbox.

I wanted their life.

FINALLY, ONE LONELY FRIDAY NIGHT I decided that I owed it to myself to give the other team a fighting chance, and went to the Rainbow Room, the local gay bar. I wasn't looking to pick anyone up, I don't think. It was more like a trial run, to see if this was a viable alternative. I mean, it clearly wasn't working with women. I'd never been attracted to a guy before, but I'd never tried, either. It seemed like it was worth a shot.

This is the kind of story that usually ends with mortifying and hilarious results. In my case, it never even got that far. The bar was filled with great-looking young guys dancing, drinking, having a fabulous time. It looked so easy.

I parked myself in a dark corner and sipped my seven-dollar beer. I don't know what I thought was going to happen, but I'd decided that anything had to be better than The Fight. I tried to ignore the terrible disco music and ogle the guys.

I was on my second beer when I realized that I couldn't keep my eyes off the few women in the place. It just wasn't happening. Thankfully, not a soul had come by to talk to me, so at least I'd been spared an attempted pick-up. It was a pathetic scene, and I knew I was wasting my time. It became obvious to me that anyone who thinks just being exposed to queer people will turn you gay is full of shit.

I abandoned the remains of my beer and stood up to leave. It was still early, by a nightclub's standards, but the place was packed and I had to weave my way through the bodies on my way out. I'd just about made it to the door when I felt a large hand on my shoulder. A jolt of panic shot through me, while a small part of my mind thought, *Finally, at least someone noticed that I'm alive.*

I turned around, trying to figure out a nice way to tell my erstwhile admirer that I was just leaving. "I'm sorry," I'd already begun when my brain froze up a little and I completely forgot what I was saying.

"Gumbo?" Johnny Frazier said, looking surprised and amused all at once. "For the life of me, I never thought I'd see you here."

"I DIDN'T THINK I'D SEE YOU HERE, EITHER," I said, a newly purchased beer in front of me, courtesy of Johnny. I'd lost touch with him in university, the same as the rest of the old crowd. I certainly never expected to find him again at the Rainbow Room.

He shrugged. "A lot of my friends are gay," he said. "I did an acting major as an undergrad. I've been hanging out here since I was nineteen — I know almost everyone in this place." He took a big slurp of his drink.

"So, are you...?" I let the question dangle, embarrassed by asking it, but it came out before I could stop myself. Johnny was cool about it, though.

"I don't like labels," he said as if that explained anything. "I'm lucky that no one at work seems to care one way or another. It's a lot more progressive than I would have thought."

I frowned. Why wouldn't the theatre be progressive? "What's your job?" I asked.

"I work for the province," he said, then seemed to remember that I didn't know anything about him anymore. "I went to law school after my undergrad. I'm a Crown prosecutor now."

I nearly spit my beer all over him. "Seriously?" I said.

He nodded. "The courtroom is great," he said. "It's just theatre for a tiny audience. I love it." He leaned toward me. "But all this is just putting off the inevitable. Tell me, Brian, what the hell are you doing alone in the Rainbow Room?"

I LEFT OUT THE GORY DETAILS, but it felt good to talk to someone about my women troubles. And I'll give him his due: Johnny didn't even laugh when I told him about my ridiculous plan to try to like guys instead. He just let me talk and then nodded sagely when I'd finally run out of steam.

"That sucks, buddy," he said. "And I sort of see how you feel. But it's not women that are the problem. It's you."

"Come on," I said. "Look around. These guys are having a great time. It's got to be easier to have a relationship with someone who gets you, right?"

"You don't really believe that Mars and Venus crap, do you?" he asked. I did, of course. But he made it sound like I was a flat-earther or something, so I just shrugged.

"People are people, Gumbo. All relationships are hard." He got a thoughtful expression on his face and something clouded in his eyes. "Trust me, gender doesn't have much to do with it."

We drank in silence for a moment, and then he grinned. "And that's why I don't even bother with 'relationships' anymore." He waggled his eyebrows in a pantomime of a leer. "Friends with benefits. Now that's where it's at."

This time I did spit beer. Johnny laughed and slapped me on the back. "I'm just fucking with you. You're all right, Gumbo. You know, we should get together again sometime." He looked around the room, which was getting louder and hotter as time went on. "I hate to admit it," he said, "but I'm getting too old for this."

After that night, Johnny and I had a nearly regular dinner date once a month. He would make me laugh with some story from court or his theatre days. I'd bore him with engineering or parents-search talk, and he'd listen when some new relationship bit the dust after The Fight, then tell me to quit bitching and get over it.

At times it felt like there had never been a point when we weren't friends, like those years between middle school and the Rainbow Room were just a momentary loss of contact. As if we'd just lost each other's numbers for a decade. As if we'd never stopped caring about each other.

23
A MATTER OF TIME

I **WAS DRIVING HOME FROM WORK** when the phone rang. I try not to answer the phone when I'm driving — it takes my concentration from the road and I never feel entirely safe. I let the call go to voice mail.

It was a Tuesday, so I stopped off at Thrifty's, then popped into the liquor store for some beer. Carrying everything, I managed to stop at the mailbox in the lobby — I was expecting a couple of DVDs from the movie rental service I used. So I was totally laden down as I rode the elevator up to my place.

I'd long since moved out of my dinky apartment in Handgun Heights. After a couple of years of a decent salary, even I had to admit that it was time for a nicer place. My new apartment was on the seventeenth floor of one of the few high-rises in town. It wasn't much bigger than my old place, but it was worlds apart in every other way: hardwood floors, oak cabinets and stainless-steel appliances in the kitchen, jets in the bathtub. It cost about double what I'd been paying, but I could afford it and I liked the place.

I set my groceries down on the island counter and started putting things away. Something nudged the back of my mind, but I couldn't remember what it was. Once the stuff was put away and I was eating my dinner of a roast chicken leg with a deli salad from the store, I remembered. That phone call.

I wiped my chickeny fingers on a napkin and grabbed my phone. I punched up voice mail and was glad I didn't have a mouthful of food when I heard the message.

"Hi, Gumbo. It's Blair. Sorry I missed you at Mom's party the other week, but you saw what it was like. Crazy. Anyway, Ange told me you two had a chat and I figured we should maybe get together sometime. If we wait too long, the baby will be here and that'll be the end of free time. So give me a call. And give me Johnny's number, too; we can make a real reunion of it. Okay, bye."

WE WENT OVER TO BLAIR AND ANGELA'S that weekend. They lived in a walk-up that reminded me more of my cheap old place than my current apartment, but it was nicely furnished, clean and a pretty good size. They had two bedrooms and were already well into the process of converting the second one into a kid's room. There was still a filing cabinet and an old tower PC in there, but they'd painted the walls light yellow with a cartoony wallpaper border, and a crib was ready to be set up in a corner. It was terrifying.

I'd brought a dozen beer and a fancy sparkling grape juice that I hoped Angela would like. It was Johnny's idea — he'd won rock paper scissors best of three and opted to bring snacks, but then told me what to buy for drinks. It was a good thing he chose to bring the food: I would have showed up with a couple of bags of chips, but Johnny brought a bunch of little canapés and desserts that he got from the gourmet deli near his condo.

"Wow," Blair said, looking at the spread Johnny laid out, "fancy stuff."

Johnny shrugged. "I've finally moved on from PB and J," he said, patting his still solid gut.

"This is a nice place," I said, looking around the apartment. "You been here long?"

"A couple of years," Angela said. "There's a good school nearby, too, so I don't see us moving soon."

"I gotta admit," Johnny said, arranging the snacks artfully on a plate Blair found for him, "it's pretty weird hearing you guys talk about schools and stuff. I mean, it still seems like just the other day *we* were in school."

"Yeah," Angela said. "I remember thinking that thirty would be so old. Like, I'd be practically dead at thirty. But I still feel like a seventeen-year-old ... or at least I did until a couple of months ago." She grinned.

"So," I said, "I don't want to be rude, but was this a planned thing?" I looked pointedly at Angela's belly. "I mean, you don't really seem like the kid types."

Blair laughed. "Things change, Gumbo," he said. "I think I've always been the kid type, really. When Debbie was little, I used to love playing with her." He turned to Johnny. "I was always envious of you, having Mary around. Little kids are so much fun."

"You've got to be kidding," Johnny said. "Shit, if I'd known I'd probably have given you every last one of my G.I. Joes to take over babysitting duty."

We all laughed. "What about you?" I asked Angela. "You going to be one of those moms with a baby strapped to your back while you get arrested for picketing the G8 summit?"

"Probably," she said, grinning. "It was kind of a hard decision, bringing a new life into this piece-of-shit world we live in." Her smile faded. "But humans survive; it's what we do. I'm trying to make the world a better place, not just roll over and volunteer for extinction." She popped a tiny quiche in her mouth. "So, to answer your question, we weren't trying, exactly, but we weren't trying not to. We're both pretty stoked about it, though. It's going to be quite a trip."

"No shit," Johnny said, sounding less than enthusiastic. "So, Blair, what is up with your mom? That party was nuts."

Angela rolled her eyes and walked off to the bathroom. "Mom," Blair said, equal parts disgust and affection in his voice. "She's got some interesting ideas. My sister Debbie just got her PhD. She's an endocrinologist — literally curing diseases for a living. And all my mother can talk about is when she's going to find a man and start pumping out kids. It's crazy. I mean, my mother's a professional herself, but none of that matters anywhere near as much as breeding."

"She must be happy with you two, then," I said.

"She's thrilled," Angela said, coming back from the bathroom. "It's just a shame she doesn't recognize anything else. I mean, all we've really done so far is screw, and you'd think we'd won a joint Nobel Prize for fixing the environmental crisis and instituting world peace. Like having children is the only purpose a person has in life and the rest is just dressing."

"I could buy it better if she'd given more of a shit about us growing up," Blair said with soft anger.

"What do you mean?" I asked. "You guys did all right."

"Sure, we had lots of stuff," Blair said. "Mom and Dad just bought us things to make up for the fact that they were never around, then that they were fighting all the time and then that they got divorced. There's more to being a good parent than throwing lavish birthday parties and Toys 'R' Us shopping sprees."

Angela reached over and squeezed Blair's shoulder. "We'll do better, honey," she said, and he nodded gravely.

"Anyway, enough of my childhood baggage. What's up with you guys?" Blair said. "Something interesting must have happened in the last decade."

"You'd think," Johnny said. "You probably heard that I'm a lawyer. I work for the province as a prosecutor. I don't do criminal trials, so don't even ask. It's not really that interesting to talk about, but I think it's fun."

"That's great," Angela said, then turned to me. "How about you?"

"I'm an engineer," I said. "I work for the city."

"Cool," Blair said, sounding less than excited.

"Oh, Gumbo's just keeping the interesting stuff under wraps," Johnny said, grinning at me. "Tell them," he said.

"What?" Angela asked.

"Well," I said, my face getting hot, "I found my birth mother."

"And that's not all," Johnny added. "She comes with a whole family. They've been hanging out." He jerked his head at me. "He even took Shirley and Dom to meet them!"

I SPENT THE NEXT HOUR FILLING BLAIR AND ANGELA IN on meeting Kim and the rest of them. Blair thought it was weird, Angela thought it was cool and Johnny was Johnny. It was Angela who brought up the elephant in the room.

"What about your father," she asked, "your birth father? You haven't mentioned anything about him."

I sighed. "She won't talk about him," I said. "Everyone I ask says they don't know anything and she's made it clear to me that the topic is off limits. He's not listed on the adoption papers and there's no record of his name on any of the hospital papers. It's maddening. I'm sure she knows who it is. I mean, she was sixteen. How many possibilities could there be?"

"Jesus, Gum," Angela said. "Has it ever occurred to you that maybe she was raped? Maybe it was a stranger and she *doesn't* know who he is."

"Or maybe it's even worse than that," Johnny said darkly. "Sounds like her family was pretty out there. You know those crazy religious people — Lot's daughters and all that."

"Okay, that's just disgusting," I said. "And I can't believe you guys are talking like this about my mother!" I heard my voice rising.

"I'm sorry, Gum," Angela said, her voice soft. "We're not trying to be offensive —" she glared at Johnny "— but it is a real possibility that there's a very good reason Kim doesn't want to talk about the man who got her pregnant."

"You'd be surprised how common it is," Blair said. "We see it at the agency time and time again — young women, abused, assaulted, becoming pregnant. It's real, Brian." He looked so earnest, like it was just the two of us in the room. I felt my heart rate go down and realized that Blair must be very good at his job. "You've got to remember that this is just as emotional for Kim as it is for you," he went on, "possibly more so. I know you want to find out about your birth father, but you've got to try to be sensitive to her situation, too."

I nodded. "Yeah, I know," I said. "It's just so hard, knowing that the information is there but I can't get at it."

"Yeah," Angela said. "But look at how much more you know now than you did a year ago. It's amazing the difference a little time can make."

"And," Johnny said, looking around the room at the empty plates and beer bottles, "sometimes how little difference it can make." The tension in the room lifted and we all smiled at each other. In the dim light of their second-hand halogen lamp I could see the reflections of all our seven-year-old faces in their eyes.

24
DEARLY BELOVED

IT WAS ONE OF THOSE SCORCHING-HOT August days we rarely get on the Island. The Civic didn't have air conditioning — I couldn't justify the additional cost for the one or two days it gets really hot. However, as I drove up island in the plus-thirty-degree heat and felt myself sweating through my shirt, I wished I'd put up the extra couple hundred bucks.

I'd booked a room at one of the local motels, knowing that the chances of staying sober at a wedding were close to nil and not wanting to impose myself on Kim's yard with another rented tent. I could cab it back and forth between the motel and the house, where the wedding and reception were taking place. Thankfully, it also meant I'd be able to change into my suit at the motel.

I pulled into the parking lot with a couple of hours to spare before I needed to be out at Kim's. I figured it was a fifteen-minute cab ride out to her place, so I shucked off my sweaty driving clothes and jumped in the shower. An hour later I looked like a new man — or at least a clean and besuited one. I had the front desk call me a cab and went down to the small lobby to wait.

I wasn't late to the wedding, but there were already a ton of people there by the time I arrived. It made the family camp-out look like a quiet night in. I almost didn't recognize Kim's place. The camping area had been redone as an outdoor chapel, with seats, an aisle and a flower-strewn covered area where I presumed the couple would be standing. I saw Rob standing near the aisle with a bunch of programs and I started walking toward him. I was a few steps away when I felt a hand on my shoulder. I turned and looked down into a face that at first I didn't recognize.

Time had been kind to her. She looked not so much older as more confident, more alive. Her hair was soft and bounced around her face wildly. She wore a burgundy pantsuit that somehow managed to look sexier than a little black dress ever could. I, on the other hand, must have looked like a moron. I'm sure my mouth was hanging open and my eyes were bugging out.

"Brian Gumbo," she said and flung her arms around me for a hug. "I don't believe it."

"I ..." I stammered. "This is ..."

"What are you doing here?" we both asked at the same time. The resulting laughter broke me out of my trance and I said, "Seedy. You look great. I can't believe it."

"I know," she said. "How weird. I'm a librarian now. I work with Terry," she explained, then lowered her voice. "And we went out before she hooked up with Chuck. I'm not exactly Chuck's favourite person, but what can you do?"

"Oh," I said, wrapping my head around what she was saying. "Oh, sure, yeah."

"So what about you?" she asked. "How do you know these guys?"

"Chuck's mom, Kim," I said, "she's my birth mother."

"No way," Seedy said, her eyes wide. "That's so twenty-first century. I'm glad you finally found her. When did you two meet?"

"A few months ago," I said.

"Whoa," Seedy said. "You move fast, pal. I don't know if I'd be joining the fam that quick."

"I'm not," I said. "But the timing just worked out ... you know. Terry invited me, really."

"Yeah, she would," Seedy said with no small amount of affection. "She's a real global community person, you know, we are all family, that kind of thing."

"Seems like it," I said and found that we'd managed to make it to the last row of seats.

"This is a strange combination," Rob said, his eyes flicking back and forth between me and Seedy.

"Gumbo and I go way back," Seedy said. "University days."

"Small world," Rob said. "So, we're not doing sides — I mean, what do you say, 'bride's side or bride's side'? So sit wherever you want back of the first couple of rows." He handed us a couple of the folded sheets that served as programs, and we walked up the aisle. I have to confess that walking up the aisle at a wedding with Seedy P next to me seemed very, very surreal.

I WASN'T REALLY SURE WHAT TO EXPECT. Neither Terry nor Chuck had seemed particularly religious, but when I flipped open the program, the officiant was listed as Rev. Jack Dorcet. The plan was for Terry and Chuck to walk down the aisle with their parents and meet at the front. Then the whole thing would probably take only a half hour before the party started. Seemed good to me.

In a few minutes I saw the little man in the brown suit from the rehearsal come to the front and stand under the canopy. He wore a suit that was obviously different from the one he'd had on previously, but for the life of me I couldn't tell you in what way. Seedy nudged me with her elbow. "Show's starting," she stage whispered.

I heard Mendelssohn's "Wedding March" being piped over a poor-quality PA and everyone rustled as they turned to look behind them. I saw Rob and Jeannette walk toward us with a man and woman I didn't recognize. My eyes skipped down to the program and saw that they were Terry's brother Andrew and her friend Elena. They reached the small man and the canopy, turned and looked expectantly down the aisle.

I turned and felt my eyes bugging out again. Terry stood with her parents, in a typically weddingy cream-coloured froth that managed to look natural on her. There must have been an entire grove of flowers woven into her hair, and she was beaming at us all. It was pretty much what I expected.

Chuck, on the other hand, was a shocker. I'd just kind of assumed she'd be wearing a pantsuit or a tux. Instead, she wore an emerald-green satin dress, strapless and snug, that hung all the way to the grass. She wasn't a tall person, but it made her look like what my mom would call a long cool drink of water. She looked stunning and she knew it. Kim stood on her left and a man I assumed was her father stood on her right.

The six of them walked slowly up the aisle, Chuck and Terry fighting not to glance at each other. I saw Terry stifle a giggle. They made it up to the rest of the wedding party, parents kissing daughters and taking their seats in the front row, leaving Chuck and Terry with no one and nothing between them. Their hands found each other and they moved closer together.

Reverend Dorcet smiled at them and at us and began.

"Family and friends of Chuck and Terry, let me welcome you to this celebration of their love and commitment to one another.

"*Family* is a word that gets a lot of press these days. Politically, family values are often code for suppressing the rights of people who chose to live and love in ways that are different from the people hoisting that phrase into the air. But the real values that make up a family — caring for one another, lifting each other up to find our full potential, sharing our material and emotional wealth — these values are central to human existence and they know no political boundary. Whenever we find people with whom we can share these values, it is cause for celebration, and we should always be supportive when our loved ones expand their own circle of family."

I saw Kim choke back a sob, and Chuck looked steadfastly at the reverend, so much so that I thought she might be trying to burn a hole in his natty suit. Terry squeezed her hand and smiled at her.

"Family is more than mere genetic relationship," the reverend went on. "Many of us find more kinship with the people we chose to include in our lives than with those to whom we are connected by blood. I am reminded that the word *love* is a verb, not simply something we acquire the same way we do our height or eye colour.

"And so, here today, we celebrate the creation of one new family and the extension and joining of two existing families. Through the commitment of these two women, Teresa and Charlotte, to a marriage that includes not only them, but by extension their other loved ones, we reaffirm the most important of all human achievements, the capacity for love."

The reverend spoke to the wedding party quietly, and I saw Rob and Terry's friend Elena reach into their pockets. Rob handed Chuck a small box. She turned toward Terry and in a soft voice began to speak.

"Terry, I promise to love and support you, in everything you choose to do. I want to carry you over the difficulties and stand beside you in your triumphs. I will be your friend, your lover, your partner in all things, for as long as love lasts." She fumbled with the box in her hand, nearly dropping it, sending Terry into a small fit of giggles. She recovered the box, opened it and took out a ring, which she slipped onto Terry's finger.

Terry took her own box from Elena and turned back to Chuck. "My darling, beautiful Charlotte," she started, and Chuck immediately began to cry. "I have loved you my whole life; my only regret is that it took me so long to find you. I will love you as long as the stars burn in the sky, as long as the trees stand in the forest. You are my heartstone, you ground me to the Earth, you let me fly. With you by my side we will live as one heart, one life together. I promise my heart to you, for always and forever." She put the ring on Chuck's finger. I heard a small sound from the front row and saw that Kim had entirely dissolved into tears.

I glanced over at Seedy, who had a smile on her face and the glint of a few tears in her own eyes. The minister then took a gnarled old broom from behind the dais, and swept a circle around Chuck and Terry. He came back to a spot between them and the guests and crouched down, holding the broom out horizontally over the ground. Holding hands, Chuck and Terry hitched up their dresses and stepped over the broom together, then turned to each other. The minister stood and said, "By the authority of the Unitarian Church of Victoria and the province of British Columbia, I introduce to you for the first time as a married couple, Charlotte and Teresa Prokopnik-Frost."

On that cue, Chuck pulled Terry close to her and they kissed for a long time while the guests whooped and clapped. When they finally pulled apart and walked down the aisle holding hands, we threw confetti and rice. I turned to Seedy. "Doesn't she look fantastic?" I asked.

"Yeah," she said a little wistfully. "She's got the whole Earth Mother thing going."

"Huh?" I said, looking back at Chuck. I noticed Terry then, the flowers in her hair bobbing as she and Chuck walked over to the table to sign the wedding licence. "No ..." I said, about to explain that I was talking about Chuck; then seeing the look on Seedy's face, I decided not to bother.

THE HOME FOR WAYWARD PARROTS

152

25
THE PARROT INCIDENT

AFTER THE SIGNING OF THE REGISTER, the proceedings took on a significantly more relaxed tone. There was a receiving line as people left the part of the yard where the ceremony had taken place, offering congratulations, hugs and kisses to the happy couple. Seedy and I were about halfway through the group, and both Chuck and Terry seemed a bit taken aback to see us together.

"Congratulations," I said, giving them each a brief hug and cheek kiss.

"Thanks," Terry said. "Do you two know each other?" she asked, looking at Seedy with confusion.

"We went out in university," she said matter-of-factly. "Gumbo was one of my groupies when I was in a punk band. Eerie coincidence, eh?"

I rolled my eyes, but smiled. "I was not a groupie," I said. "Not at first, anyway."

Chuck's eyes darted from me to Seedy and back again; then she grinned. "It's good to see you," she said and winked at me salaciously when Seedy's back was turned. "Weddings are great for rekindling old flames," she whispered, and I felt my face colour.

I felt the press of the rest of the line behind me, so had to move on before I could protest my intentions. After all, Seedy seemed to have moved on from men, and anyway, I found it hard to believe that we'd be able to go back in time.

Though as I was thinking this, I felt Seedy grab my hand and pull me toward her. "Let's find the bar," she said and dragged me off toward the group of small tented tables. There was an hour before dinner, so we had a couple of drinks and chatted. It was nice talking to Seedy again.

"We'd better find our tables," I said, not wanting to leave her.

"Sure," she said and walked over to the poster-sized master list. She squinted at it, then poked me in the side. "I bet there's room at your table. I'll just come sit with you." Before I could protest, she dragged me off to our table and commandeered one of the seats.

"Hi," she said, turning to the people seated on her right. "Hope you don't mind if I just barge in here." I recognized the couple and sat down next to Seedy.

I grinned at Michael and Marita. "This is my old friend, Celia-Dee. She's a friend of Terry's and we just happened to run into each other. You mind if she joins us?"

"Not at all," Marita said. "It's a small world, isn't it?"

I was just about to explain to Seedy who Michael and Marita were when we heard an amazing racket coming from the tent where the buffet was being laid out. The noise level increased and soon was accompanied by a round of very loud, high-pitched screaming.

I was starting to wonder if someone was being murdered when I saw a blur of red, green and grey. "Oh, god," I said to Seedy. "Someone let Napoleon out."

IT WASN'T AS BAD AS IT COULD HAVE BEEN. It turned out that Napoleon, mean as he was, was scared of freedom and stayed mostly up in the rafters of the rental tent. Of course, his activities up there weren't going to make the party supply company too happy. By the time we got to the tent, he'd chewed a metre-wide hole in the canvas, shreds dropping down like confetti on the buffet table. Which wasn't so bad, really — it covered the blobs of parrot guano he was also dropping with prodigious regularity.

I think Napoleon's greatest contribution to the melee wasn't the shit or the shred. It was the volume. "Idiot," squawked the big bird, in a voice that carried well over the shrieks and snickers of the guests. "Ugh. Idiot. Squawk."

"What the fuck is that?" Seedy said when we got back to the site of the disaster.

"Someone let the parrots out," I said dumbly. "They're not very nice birds, either. I doubt that's the only one. We should maybe hide."

"Are you crazy?" she said. "This is hilarious. Ow!"

She jumped back and I saw the big grey, Peter Piper, flapping away from her. A small red line of blood welled up on her neck where the bird had scratched her. "I take it back," she said. "I'm with you on the hiding."

I never knew which bird it was — it didn't sound like Napoleon; I'd gotten to know his voice — but over all the other sounds came a very crisp and clear, but definitely avian, "Motherfucker! Cunt-assed fuckstick. Squawk."

"Okay," I said as we continued our retreat, "that was pretty funny."

I steered her into the house and found a free bathroom. I cleaned her cut and rooted around in the cupboards for a bandage. "What's with all those birds?" she asked.

"Kim works at a pet store," I explained. "And she takes the bad birds home so they don't get destroyed. There's a whole room full of them. I guess the door got opened somehow and a bunch got out. Poor Kim."

"Poor Kim?" Seedy said. "Poor Chuck and Terry. Talk about ruining their day."

"I dunno," I said. "It's going to be pretty memorable, and that's a good thing, so long as no one loses an eye." That made Seedy laugh and I felt a pang of something in my gut. Nostalgia maybe, or regret — it was hard to say. She sure did look good in that suit, though.

"Anyway," I said, moving away from her in the small room. "We'd better go. There's probably a whole line of gashes and scrapes waiting to get in here." She smiled at me and we went back out to the yard.

BY THE TIME WE GOT OUTSIDE, the parrots had been contained. Someone had cleaned up the buffet table and was getting food out. I saw Chuck at one of the tables talking to a man I didn't recognize, a huge smile on her face. I guessed that I was right about the birds adding more colour than trouble to the festivities, at least in her eyes. She was used to them, after all.

As wedding receptions go, it was probably up there. I don't remember much of the one other wedding I'd been to, but from what I could guess, this one was more fun than the mean. I danced with a half dozen women, including Seedy, only stopping for a drink every now and again.

I must have been getting pretty drunk and all the people were starting to get to me. I was at the bar talking to Jeannette about the Facebook incident.

"I probably shouldn't have posted that," she said, "but I'm sick of them getting away with spewing their shit all over us." She took a swig of her drink, some kind of juice and booze number, I guessed. "Chuck disowned them after what they said to Terry." I was curious, but could probably guess. "It's tough," she went on, "because Mom still talks to them. I mean, they completely fucked up her life ..." She stopped short and stared at me with a shocked look on her face. "I'm sorry, Brian, I didn't mean ..."

"It's okay," I said. "Kim told me about her parents' reaction to ... well, me."

"Anyway," Jeannette went on, her face a bright red, "they're just awful, but Mom still loves them. I just didn't want anyone else to get blindsided by their nastiness."

"I get it," I said, and we stood together in companionable silence for a moment. Finally, she touched my arm and said, "Thanks for letting me vent," then wandered off. I found myself alone at the bar, strangers all around me. I've never been good in that situation and, between the conversation and my not inconsiderable tipsiness, I was feeling particularly in need of getting out of there. I grabbed a nearby bottle of wine and started walking to a part of the yard that seemed to be less crowded. The sound of the DJ faded, the laughter and murmurs of voices grew dim, and then I saw a small flickering light from a corner of the yard. I walked that way and found Wolf leaning up against a tree, smoking a cigarette.

"Mind if I join you?" I asked.

He smiled and said, "Nice to have the company," and offered me an open pack of cigarettes.

"No, thanks," I said. "I'm here for the break, not the smoke."

He shrugged and put the pack back in his breast pocket. "You're not used to the mob yet," he said.

"No," I said. "It's always just been me and Mom and Dad. I've never really been good at crowds."

"This bunch can be a bit more challenging than most," he said, dragging deeply on his cigarette. "I love them, that's for sure. But Kim's always been her own person, and the crazy family she's created doesn't follow the program in a lot of ways." I started to realize that he was at least as drunk as I was. "I hope you don't expect too much of them, especially her. She's wasn't always this way ..." He stubbed out the cigarette in a pot with a dead plant in it. "But Kim's kind of ... I don't know ... fickle. She gets really excited about new things, then loses interest just as fast. I just don't want you to think ..."

"It's okay," I said. "I never expected anything from her, really. I just wanted to know, you know? I've already gotten a lot more from her than I hoped to." I scowled into the darkness. "Except ..."

"What?" Wolf asked, lighting another cigarette. I pulled the bottle of wine out of my pants pocket where I'd managed to stow it while I was walking around. I took a drink straight from the bottle, then passed it to him. He shook his head, took a pull from a bottle of Guinness, then repeated, "What?"

"I was hoping to find out who my father was," I said. "I get the feeling it's not a happy memory — no one seems to know anything, and Kim won't talk about it."

"Yeah," Wolf said, taking another swig. "That."

"You know something?" I asked.

"No," he said. "I don't know anything. I just ..."

"What?" I asked, my voice rising.

"Never mind," he said, a lawyerly tone of finality in his voice.

"No," I said. "If you know something, tell me, please. Kim doesn't need to know ..."

"Not now," he said. "I have to think about it. I'm sorry, Brian. Just give me some time. I promise I'll get back to you, I just can't ... I'm too drunk now."

"Damn it," I said, but without malice.

He put his hand on my shoulder. "Yeah," he said. "Damn it."

AFTER THAT I FINISHED THE REST OF THE BOTTLE of wine and spent the remainder of the evening dancing, drinking and grazing on what was left of the buffet table. Seedy found me after an hour or two, as worse for wear as I was feeling.

"I can't drive home," she announced, flopping down into a chair next to me.

"No," I agreed, "you can't."

"Wanna split a cab?"

"I'm not going back to town," I said. "I planned ahead and got a motel room in Maple Bay."

"Smart guy," Seedy said. "So, wanna split a cab?" She looked at me and I recognized the look in her eyes.

"Uh," I said, with as much aplomb as I ever had with her.

"Great," she said, trying to stand up and managing to pull it off on the second try. She grabbed my hand. "Let's go."

SHE HAD LEARNED A THING OR TWO in the ten years since we'd last been in bed together. I guess I probably had too, but like always she was in charge. Obviously, I hadn't planned on going to bed with anyone that night, so I was ill prepared. I was almost as surprised when Seedy pulled a bunch of condoms out of her purse as I had been by the fact that she wanted to use them with me. There was a lot more going on with this woman than I'd ever imagined.

The morning was slow to come. My head was pounding and I woke to the sound of puking in the bathroom. Thankfully, the morning after had never been one of my problems, so Seedy's troubles didn't start me off, too. She came out of the bathroom looking surprisingly good for someone who'd just been tossing her cookies.

"Morning, sunshine," she said, slipping back into the bed. "That was pretty fun yesterday, huh?"

I wasn't sure exactly what she was referring to, but regardless it was easy for me to answer, "Sure was."

It took us another hour to finally get out of bed, and we spent longer in the shower than was strictly necessary for hygiene. "I should drive you back to your car," I said after I'd checked out.

"Thanks," she said. "Wanna get breakfast first?"

"Yes," I said. "I do."

26
SUNDAY MORNING COMING DOWN

WE PULLED INTO WANG'S, which was not, as its name implied, a Chinese food restaurant. It was, rather, the best diner between Victoria and Nanaimo, at least according to the sign in its window.

The place was crowded — Sunday morning is probably the busiest time for a place like that — but we managed to slip into a small two-person booth without waiting. There were laminated menus propped between the sugar rocket and the salt and pepper shakers, and I pulled them out. It was typical diner food: exactly what we needed.

A waitress who looked like she'd been working there since the dawn of time came by with a coffee pot and took our orders. I sipped the hot coffee and looked through the steam at Seedy. She was wearing her suit from the previous night, but managed not to look ridiculous. Her cheeks were flushed and there were bags under her eyes, but the combination somehow made her look more beautiful. Maybe I was still just in shock from the surprise of seeing her — so much of her — again.

"So tell me," she said. "What are you doing these days?"

I told her about my job, and she acted more interested than most people bother to. "And you?" I asked. "You're a librarian. How is that?"

"I like it," she said. "I tried a few other things first. After I university I went to Japan and taught English for a year. Paid off my student loan, and discovered that I really do not like teaching. Came back here, did some odd jobs. And I mean strange, not just random."

"Like what?" I asked.

"I was a copy editor for an anarchist magazine for a while," she said, "and I worked the counter at a porno shop. Other stuff. It was okay; it paid the rent, but it wasn't enough. So I went back to school. That's where I met Terry, getting my MLS."

"You're a realtor?" I asked, confused.

"No," she laughed. "Master's of Library Science. Librarian school."

"You need a master's to be a librarian?"

"I know," she said, "it's pretty crazy. But everyone and their dog has a degree now, so they have to make it harder. It was a pain, but it was worth it. I love working at the library. All those books ... plus, I get to be so orderly." She made the last word sound like something dangerous and sexy. "You'd love it," she added salaciously.

I should have known that Seedy could make me blush just by talking about cataloguing books.

"So you met Terry at school?" I changed the subject.

"Yeah," she said. "We were in the same class — she went straight for her MLS after undergrad. We were an item for a couple of years in grad school."

"A couple of years," I repeated. "Wow. That's serious."

She shrugged. "We never lived together or anything," she said. "But, yeah, I loved her. Still, we weren't that great together. It was one of those intense relationships — lots of fighting and lots of making up. Fun, but not really good in the long term."

"You seem to care about her."

"I do," she said. "I'll probably always love Terry, but as much as it pains me to say it, she and Chuck were meant for each other. I'm just glad that she's happy."

Our food arrived then and we were saved from more deep talk by mountains of hash browns, stacks of toast and a mess of eggs. We ate like we'd not seen food in weeks.

THE HOME FOR WAYWARD PARROTS

IT WAS A STRANGELY FAMILIAR FEELING, eating breakfast with Seedy. Funny, since we rarely had breakfast together when we'd dated before — we rarely had the opportunity to spend the whole night together. Yet as I sat across from her at Wang's dipping toast corners into egg yolk, it was like déjà vu. We finally finished all the food, drank more coffee than necessary and split the cheque. She slipped into the passenger seat of the Civic and I drove back to Kim's so she could pick up her car.

"So," I said, as I stopped in Kim's driveway next to Seedy's old beater, "can I, uh, call you sometime?"

"You'd better," she said, grinning. She pulled out her phone and said, "Squirt me your details."

I fumbled in my pockets for my phone and we spent more time connecting our devices and sharing contact files than it would have taken to write down our numbers. But there was no excuse for getting digits wrong or losing the paper this way. I guessed she really did want me to call.

She waved as she got into her car, and I winced as the engine barely cranked into life. She roared off in a hail of gravel and exhaust, and I was about to follow when I saw movement from the corner of my eye. Kim came out the front door, a large blue-and-green parrot on her arm. She waved at me and motioned for me to come inside. I turned off the car and stepped gingerly onto her driveway. An uncaged parrot made me as wary now as I imagined a similarly unrestrained tiger would.

Kim must have seen the trepidation on my face because she said, "Oh, don't worry about Bluebeard here. He's not violent, just ugly." She turned to go back into the house and I saw that the other side of the bird was missing about half the proper number of feathers. Mottled skin showed through in nasty-looking patches, and one of the beast's feet seemed to have far too many talons. Kim wasn't kidding — that was one ugly bird.

I followed Kim and Bluebeard though the door and made my way to the kitchen while she stowed the bird. I sat at the small table and when Kim returned she offered me a coffee. My caffeine needle was pointing at the F, but I accepted a cup anyway. "I see you met someone at the wedding," she said, a sly smile on her face.

I blushed, but said, "Not really. We knew each other from before. Just a weird coincidence."

"Hrm," Kim said. "I'm not really a big believer in coincidences. Looks like you rekindled something, eh?"

I shrugged. Talking about this with Kim was more uncomfortable than usual, which was saying a lot. I never liked talking about the women I liked. Perhaps it was my discomfort that prompted me to find another topic of conversation. I remembered my brief chat with Wolf the night before.

"So, Kim," I started, looking intently at my coffee cup. "I know you don't want to talk about who my father is, and I respect that. But finding him, even if it's only a name, isn't just curiosity for me. I can imagine a lot of reasons why you wouldn't want to talk about him with the rest of them, and why you wouldn't want to tell me anything. But please," I lifted my eyes to hers, "please don't stand in my way of finding out for myself."

I thought she would cut me off again or, worse, start to cry. Instead she said nothing, and I sat there for what seemed like forever, my heart pounding. Finally, she took a sip from her own cup and said, "You know, everyone thinks they're anti-social or just plain bad. But they aren't malicious — I'm confident that none of those birds wants to hurt anyone. They're just operating without some basic information."

I didn't know what got her started talking about the birds, but I just didn't have the energy to force the conversation back to my father. So I let her go on. "I don't know what happened to him, but Napoleon — he's afraid. That's why he attacks people: he's just defending himself. He doesn't know that we're not the ones who hurt him. And Peter Piper, I think he doesn't understand that we're not all parrots. He's protecting his territory. They aren't bad birds, they're just ... missing something. Maybe they forgot, or they never knew. Or maybe it's easier for them if they just ignore certain things, maybe it lets them see the world in a way that makes it easier to bear what they've lost."

I'd lost where she was going with this conversation, but as abruptly as she started this strange monologue about bird psychology, she changed tacks again. "You should call Wolfie sometime," she said. "I bet the two of you would have lots to talk about. I'll give you his number." She got up and opened a drawer. She rifled through the papers, rubber bands and plastic bags that filled the drawer until she found a stubby pencil and a scrap of an old receipt. She wrote some numbers on the back and handed it to me.

She looked at me expectantly and I didn't know what she wanted. So I stood, thanked her for the coffee, told her the wedding had been lovely and left.

27
SEEING YOU AGAIN

October 22, 1980
Dear kimmie,

    I thought it would be hot here, but it's
not that bad. We're on the coast, I'm not
allowed to tell you where exactly, but it's
almost like being at home except everything is
dusty and brown and there aren't any trees.
Not real trees, anyway.

    It's kind of boring here now. There's no
fighting and all we do all day is clean. But I
just keep thinking of all the money I'm making
and not spending and that makes it all Ok.

    Write to me. Letters are the most exciting
thing that happens here. I miss you.

    Jim

I CALLED SEEDY A WEEK AFTER THE WEDDING, expecting her to laugh in my face. But she surprised me as always.

"Gumbo!" she said instead of hello. "I was just going to call you."

"Well, for once I beat you to something," I said, and she laughed.

"I was just thinking that we had a pretty good time the other night," she said. "We should do that some more, don't you think?"

"Go to weddings?"

"Ha! No, the wedding part wasn't what I was talking about. You free this weekend sometime?"

"Sure," I said, thinking, *Am I really being propositioned by my old girlfriend?*

"How about dinner?" she asked.

"Why not," I said. "We have to eat, right?"

"Right," she said. "Give me your address and I'll pick you up at seven on Friday."

"Sure," I agreed again, wondering how things had happened so quickly again. Seedy. She always knew how to get me to do what she wanted. I liked that about her.

SHE TOOK ME TO A KOREAN PLACE I'd never seen before, which was so fancy I started to panic slightly when we arrived. I could afford it, I knew, but why would she take me somewhere so nice? I didn't know what most of the things on the menu were, but Seedy seemed to know the place well. She ordered a half dozen items for us and then played with the stainless-steel chopsticks while we waited.

"I often wondered about you," she said as we sipped warm sake, "how things were for you after we split up."

"You knew where I was," I said.

She shook her head. "Yeah," she said, "but I was too young then. I didn't know that when you fuck up, you just stand up, admit that you did and move on."

"What do you mean?"

"I didn't break up with you because anything changed between us," she said, sounding exasperated. "I broke up with you because everything else in my life was changing. I figured that you and me belonged with the rest of it and that when things change, they all change. I didn't know any better. It wasn't fair and I'm sorry."

That was the moment our silent-but-deadly waiter chose to appear out of thin air and separate us with the steaming and chilled dishes Seedy had ordered. Looking at them, I still couldn't tell what most were, but the smells that rose from them were all delicious. I seemed to have lost my appetite, however.

Seedy dug into the plates of food, serving herself generous portions of everything. I didn't move. There was a knot of something building in my chest. Hurt, anger — it was like all the rejection I'd ever felt was coalescing into an arterial blockage. A heart attack of a different kind.

Finally, while she was tasting her second choice, I found my voice. "Is that what this is?" I said. "An apology for dumping me ten years ago? Is that what last weekend was, too? One final fuck before you kiss me off properly?"

She set her chopsticks down carefully and looked at me. "No," she said sadly. "That's not what this is. This is — or at least this was — a date. I was just talking about the past because, you know, it's what we have in common. And it's something that bugged me all this time. And I figured that after ten years, we'd both be able to see our past more clearly." She picked up her chopsticks again, but didn't take a bite of anything. "I guess I was wrong."

I frowned, not understanding. But that knot in my chest broke apart, and I could feel an almost physical dissolution of something toxic that had filled me. It was like I was a barrel full of pain and she'd poked a hole in me. Slowly it drained away.

After a minute, I served myself from the dishes in the centre and ate. Everything was delicious. After I'd tried it all, I said, "I'm sorry, Seedy. I don't really get it, but ... well ... I thought about you a lot, too. After, I mean."

She smiled at me with a mouthful of gyoza. After she'd swallowed, she said, "I can't stay mad at you, Gumbo. You're not like other people and that's what I've always liked about you. How can I expect you to ..." She saw me looking confused again and laughed. "It's okay. Really. Don't worry about it."

I took a bite of something saucy and hot and chewed. "So," I said, after a pause, "is this a date again, then?"

AFTER SEEDY LEFT THE NEXT MORNING, I fished out the scrap of paper Kim had given me. I knew that Wolf had answers for me, even if he didn't want to give them up. And I wanted them, I really did. But every time I was about to call him, this voice in the back of my mind asked me what I would do if I found out that my father was a rapist. For god's sake, he could have been a child molester. What if I was a product of incest? What if Kim had some horrible uncle who'd been hurting her her whole life until she finally got pregnant? What if she never told anyone her secret because she was afraid? Afraid for herself. Afraid for me. Did I really want to know that?

So I'd carried around the shiny Canadian Tire receipt all week, worrying it like some ancient stone as I walked the Inner Harbour on my lunch breaks. It caught the light as it sat next to my laptop in the evenings, and my eyes glanced over to it while I meant to focus on *Ghost in the Shell* or some DVD episode of *Firefly*. It was a talisman and it was a burden.

I could still smell Seedy's body on my skin. I wasn't exactly surprised when she'd followed me in after dinner and we'd ended up in bed again. It was nice to be sober this time; hell, it was just plain nice. After the rocky start to the meal, things had smoothed out, and I had to admit that I was happier than I'd been in years.

We'd talked about Seedy's job (making order out of chaos) and my job (making order out of chaos), books and movies we'd enjoyed and more amusingly the ones we'd hated, the most recent election. It was like meeting someone new without all the getting-to-know-you garbage. It was fun.

Back at my place was also fun, and also familiar and strange at the same time. In the morning, I found some granola in the back of the cupboard, remembering how she practically used to live off the stuff stirred into a cup of yogourt. I brought her a bowl back to the bed, and she laughed, the sound tinkling in my ears. "I haven't eaten this in years," she said, taking a huge spoonful. "I can't imagine why not. This is fantastic."

As she was leaving, she asked if I wanted to see her again. "Of course," I said, confused.

"I mean, you know ..." she said, suddenly shy. "I mean, do you want to be seeing me, like, regularly?"

"Are you asking me to go steady?"

She laughed, but it was kind of a nervous laugh. "That sounds dumb," she said. "I guess we'll just have to see."

"Yes," I said. "I want to see you again." She kissed me, then shut my apartment door in my face. I shook my head. I'll never understand her, I thought, but who needs understanding?

I was remembering the look in her eyes as the door closed when I thought about my conversation with Wolf. I didn't understand that either, but I knew now that whatever he had to tell me, I wanted to know it. I found the receipt in the pile of things by my laptop. The phone number had already burned itself into my memory, but I read over the digits scratched in Kim's loopy handwriting anyway. I closed my eyes, took a deep breath and reached for my phone.

28
LETTERS FROM CYPRUS

October 30, 1980

Happy Halloween! The boys are planning
a party here at the base but the rumour is
that the major is going to shut it down. I
hope not, it's been nothing but sit around and
wait since I got here. It's not that I want
another Nicosia or anything, just that it
feels like we're not doing anything. I could use
a party. We all could.

Remember the Halloween party at Dave's
last year? You told your folks you were staying with your brother and when you came home
with wine on your breath they didn't let you

out of the house for a month. It was worth it, though, what a great night. You looked so good in your Marilyn Monroe dress, I was the luckiest guy at the party. I was always the luckiest guy.

I hope your letters are just slow. I can't wait to hear from you. I miss you.

Jim

"KIM TOLD ME TO EXPECT YOUR CALL." Wolf Heinz wasn't exactly all business, but it didn't feel like a chat between buddies either. I'd seen him on TV once or twice during some flashy trial, and Johnny talked about him all the time. He was a hard-ass, a real pro, a killer in the courtroom. I'd never seen any of that in person, though. He was just Uncle Wolf: stout drinker, secret cigarette smoker, potential keeper of the identity of my father. It had always been easy to talk to him before. But now that I wanted something from him, I guess it was no more Mister Nice Guy.

"We had a kind of strange conversation," I tried to explain. "Honestly, I don't know what she was trying to tell me, but she said I should call you and gave me your number. I think she wants you to tell me what you know about my father."

I heard him sigh. "She wants me to tell you about the letters," he said.

There was a pause after which I expected him to explain, but nothing happened. "Letters?" I prompted.

"Look, Brian," he said. "I want to get something straight with you. Kim never told me who your father is. As far as I know, she's never told anyone. So I can't answer the question you're asking. But ..."

"But what?" I asked.

"Look," Wolf said. "Why don't we meet for a drink sometime this week? It's quiet right now at the courthouse and this would probably be a lot easier explained over a beer."

I didn't want to wait any more and couldn't see how a beer could possibly change what Wolf would have to say. But I had to admit that the man was intimidating and he held all the cards. He had the information I wanted and he knew it. So if he wanted to meet for a drink after work, a drink after work was what it would have to be.

SMITH'S IS A VERY STRANGE PUB. It used to be the Old Bailey, a classic English-style office workers' ginmill. When it changed hands, they kept the dark wood panelling, the long shiny bar and general ambiance. But they added an open-plan DJ booth with a pair of turntables, plush couches and microbrew on tap. At five thirty on a Wednesday afternoon, though, it was still a white-collar drinker's haven.

I sat at a low table on one of the couches, nursing a pint of Blue Truck and trying not to fidget. I'd finished half my beer when I saw him darken the doorway, his thousand-dollar suit creased after a day of doing whatever Crown prosecutors do when they aren't wearing a wig. He saw me, waved briefly, then walked directly to the bar.

In a few minutes he was sipping a pint the colour of strong coffee and walking toward me. I felt the last few sips of my own beer threatening to return. I stood.

"Thanks for coming," I said, and we both sat.

"It was my idea," he reminded me and took another long pull from his pint. He set it down on the low table between us and the faint whiff of chocolate hit my nose.

"Let me tell you a story," he said.

"LIVING IN OUR HOUSE WAS LIKE LIVING IN THE PAST," he started. "Our parents were good people, really. They loved us, in their way, and they did everything they thought was right for us. They really did believe that family was the most important thing. The trouble was, they also believed that most of history — the Scientific Revolution, the Enlightenment — well, it just didn't apply to them. They would have fit in just fine in the sixteenth century, but in nineteen seventy-nine, it was plain embarrassing.

"Kim and I did what we could to avoid the religious craziness, but they were our parents and we had to live there. That meant we were both looking for a way out as soon as we could get it." He took another long drink of his beer and peered into its dark depths.

"I wondered a lot about what might have happened if I'd stayed," he said. "Maybe Kim would have talked to me, maybe she could have done something ... But she was on her own; she was only sixteen. I can't imagine what it would have been like for her, realizing that she was pregnant, knowing what that would mean for our parents. I ... I should have been there."

He sighed and stared off at a point that was long ago and far away. "But I wasn't. As soon as I was done high school, I left to go to university. I had good grades. I got a partial scholarship, and our folks paid the rest. For all their backwardness, they believed in education and I went out and got one. I left the Island as soon as I could and came back only once a month to get a cheque for school fees in exchange for a lecture on sin. So I was free, more or less. Which is why the letters came to me.

"The Island was smaller then; we pretty much lived in the country. Everyone knew everyone, so I knew who Jim Connor was. He was a year behind me in school, a big burly kid. Seemed nice enough. It wasn't much of a surprise to anyone when he joined the Army right after high school. In those days everyone was doing a tour in Cyprus and Jim's battalion went over in the fall. September or October, I guess it was.

"I didn't know that Jim and Kim even knew each other, but then the letters started coming for her. Postmarked UN Forces Cyprus, addressed to Kim Heinz at my dorm at UBC. She never even mentioned it to me, but I understood well enough. I never opened the letters, just saved them up. On my monthly trips home I'd find some way to pass them on to Kim without my parents knowing. She just thanked me and took them. That was it.

"We never talked about it, but I guessed he was her boyfriend. At the beginning he wrote every week, then the letters slowed down until, after a couple of months, they just stopped. I didn't think much of it; I mean, teenage love doesn't generally survive long absences. And then it was obvious that Kim was pregnant and I figured — well, what could he do, halfway around the world? She was on her own and, letters or no letters, that's how it was.

"I know it sounds harsh, but eventually I forgot all about them. After ... after you were born, Kim kind of hid out for a while. But then she turned eighteen and moved out of the house, and soon she was living with Aaron. Jim Connor kind of just vanished from my mind."

He downed the remaining liquid in his glass and turned back to face the bar. He caught the barkeep's eye and lifted his glass in a signal for a refill. The young woman behind the bar nodded her understanding and started pulling the pint. He turned back to face me.

"I found out only a few weeks ago ..." he said, his voice trailing off.

"Found out what?" I asked, my own voice hoarse.

"Kim called me, asked me to tell you about the letters. So I asked her, 'This is about Jim Connor, right?' She exploded, told me never to say his name, that I had no right to talk about him, that she never wanted to hear his name again. Kim never yells. I don't think I'd ever heard her get angry like that. I just said okay and we hung up, but then later I googled him. It wasn't all that hard to find; the Canadian military keeps good records.

"Jim Connor died in Cyprus in January of 1981."

29
CASUALTIES OF WAR

November 10, 1980
Dear Kimmie,

I finally got your letters! Four all at once,
I don't know how the military mail system
works. Probably the same as everything else
here. Slow.

The Halloween party happened after all,
but it was just the guys from the base. It's
not like there's a costume store, so most of
us just dressed up in sheets. It was a party
full of ghosts and Greeks. Someone bought
a bunch of bottles of ouzo and retsina, god
I can't believe these people drink this stuff.

It's terrible, but we drank it anyway. It was pretty fun.

They told us that we're getting leave in January, but it's not enough time to come home. Just a week on the mainland. I'm sure it will be fun, but I'd rather be coming home. I'd rather be with you than sitting on a beach in Greece drinking ouzo any day. But if they're only giving us a beach in Greece then that's what I'll take!

My tour is over in April and I'm trying not to count the days, it's too long. But April isn't that far away. Write more soon!

Jim

WOLF'S SECOND BEER ARRIVED and he handed me a crisp page printed off the internet about James Masterson Connor. It was the official military notice of his death and I found that my eyes swam when I looked at it. I couldn't say a word.

"I'm sorry, Brian," he said, finally. "Kim never said that Jim was your father, but it seems likely. I never read the letters, so I don't know if he even knew or what. I don't know if they were a couple or just ... you know. But he was certainly important to her — then and, obviously, even now. Maybe this will help you find what you need, but I wouldn't expect much more from Kim. I'm surprised that she told you as much as she did."

"I ..." I stumbled for something to say. "Thank you for this, Wolf," I said finally. "I know this put you in an awkward position with Kim and I really appreciate it."

"Hey," he said, "she asked me to talk to you. I put myself in the soup, even though I didn't know it would happen." He sipped his beer and took on a thoughtful look. "Makes me wonder how much I really know about my sister. She always seems like such an open book, so it's easy to forget that hidden chapter."

"Thank you," I said again and stood. The papers were still in my hand, and I carefully pocketed them so I could shake Wolf's hand. "I have to go."

He nodded, and shook my hand. "I understand. I hope I'll see you again, Brian."

I nodded meaninglessly and left the bar, half a beer still on the table between us.

WHEN I GOT TO MY BUILDING I realized that I couldn't remember anything about driving home. I walked into my apartment, locking the door behind me, and went into the kitchen. I felt like a robot on autopilot as I took my jacket off and hung it up, then poured a glass of water. I had a name. James Masterson Connor. It was, as Johnny and no doubt Wolf would say, entirely circumstantial. There was no proof; only Kim could say for sure, and she wasn't going to. But I knew it. I knew as soon as I heard it. Jim Connor was my father.

I spent the next few nights on various Canadian Forces websites, on the Wikipedia pages for Canadian UN peacekeeping missions, learning everything I could about Jim Connor and by extension the Canadian missions in Cyprus. I was surprised to discover that we still had people there. I'd only ever vaguely known about the missions there, and you never hear anything about it anymore — it's all Afghanistan all the time now. But there are still a handful of Canadian soldiers out in the Mediterranean, now literally keeping the peace.

Shortly before Jim Connor got there, though, it wasn't so much peacekeeping as it was peace*making*. If that. There had been several Canadian casualties in the late seventies and a few deaths, but nothing in 1981. But I found a local newspaper article from back then with the lurid headline "Local Peacekeeper Dead in Cyprus." The headline made it sound like some kind of enemy attack was to blame, but the actual cause of death of the man I was now thinking of as my father was much more mundane. It turned out that he died in a car crash.

He was on his way to the airport, not as a repeat of the heroics of 1974 or even for some exercise or drill. He was on his way to catch a plane for Greece and a week's R and R. From the article it sounded like the road wasn't in great shape, but otherwise it was just one of those things. A civilian vehicle crossed the middle line and ploughed into the car driven by a staff officer named Gray and carrying my father. Gray was pulled from the wreckage with two broken legs; the driver of the civilian car was killed on impact. My father was thrown from the car and found in a ditch with a broken neck. He was pronounced dead at the scene. It was January 11, 1981, and he was less than a month away from his nineteenth birthday.

WHEN SEEDY CALLED, I told her what I'd learned from Wolf and from the internet. "You should try to track down some of the guys he served with," she said. "If Kim won't tell you about him, I bet they would."

"How would I do that?" I asked, feeling a strange sensation in my gut.

"Come on, Gumbo," she said. "You've been hunting for people all your life, people who didn't really want to be found. There must be a list of the soldiers on one of those websites you've been looking at. How hard would it be to find one or two of them now?"

"I guess," I said, wondering why I felt so reluctant to contact one of these men who knew Jim Connor back when he was just a fresh-faced recruit. They would be, what, fifty, fifty-five now? Would they even remember a guy who didn't make it through a six-month tour?

"What are they going to know, anyway?" I argued. "He might not have known about me and even if he did, there's no reason he would have talked about it to the guys in the barracks. What's the point?"

"What's the point?" Seedy echoed back at me incredulously. "What's ever been the point of looking for these people? Your mom and dad loved you, they still love you, it's obvious to anyone. You had a great set of parents, trust me. If you're just trying to figure out your chances of losing your hair, then fine, but you have to admit that there's never really been much of a logical point to this search of yours. It's just curiosity, Gumbo. And that weird evolutionary need to know our kin. But there's never been a point. You just want to know them. And the only way you're going to know this Tim O'Connor ..."

"Jim Connor," I corrected automatically.

"Yeah, Jim Connor," she said. "The only way you can get to know him is through the people who knew him then. And besides Kim, that's got to be his army pals. So. Find them. Buy them beers and pool games and meat-draw tickets at the Legion. If you really want to know, that's how you can find out."

SHE WAS RIGHT, OF COURSE. About all of it. But I didn't want to admit that my life's obsession to find my roots was really no different than being into collecting stamps or amateur rocketry. And I realized that I didn't really want to know if my father was some jerk who knocked up his underage girlfriend, then ran off to the army. Before I met Kim, it never really occurred to me that the people who were responsible for me being born could be *anyone*: they could be criminals or mentally ill, they could be assholes or worse. Before I finally found her, I always imagined tearful reunions, heartfelt apologies and nice smiling faces that reminded me eerily of Mom and Dad.

Now, though, I realized that other people aren't all like my family. They aren't even like my friends' families. I was just lucky that Kim is a genuinely kind and generous person and that her family was so welcoming. It didn't have to go that way.

I'VE NEVER LIKED INTERACTING WITH STRANGERS. For someone who spent his life looking for a specific set of strangers that probably seems odd, but it always made sense to me. My natural parents aren't strangers, exactly. I have a clear relationship with them, and meeting Kim and her family was, if not easy, at least straightforward enough with respect to who I was and how I fit in. Proper strangers, on the other hand, have none of those clear cues.

When you meet someone for the first time, you have all these things you need to figure out. How do we relate to one another? Who is more powerful, more important? Do we share the same views on things, will we argue or get along? What about our temperaments? Will they match? And I hate all of that. The not knowing.

So I didn't want to look for these men who once, long ago, knew a guy named Jim Connor who had the dumb luck to get into a car wreck on his way to a week's leave. I didn't want to have to introduce myself, explain what I wanted and listen to them judge me silently as they told me whatever they wanted to. But Seedy was right. If I wanted to know anything about Jim Connor, these were the people to ask. So I started digging.

30
THE LADY KILLER

November 19, 1980
Dear Kimmie,

I'm finally doing stuff around here. They've got me firing the anti-tank guns and man is that ever fun. Those things make the biggest noise I've ever heard and what an explosion! It's pretty awesome.

My bunkie is this guy named Dave from Nanaimo. He's only a few years older than me but he's married already and his wife just had a baby. All he wants to do is call home and talk about the kid. It's kind of sweet, but it's getting annoying. Married at 20?! Can you believe it?

I hope your letters get here soon. I miss you.

    Jim

DAVID PRESTON LOOKED EXACTLY THE WAY I imagined a career army man to look: flat-top haircut, pressed khakis and a brand-new-looking navy blue polo shirt. Solid, sensible shoes. Neat, orderly and terrifying. However, it turned out that Preston's army career had sputtered early. He had been a regular forces man during his tour in Cyprus on the pay-for-school plan. But he'd left as soon as his required years of service were over and joined the private sector as a software programmer.

He was the absolute opposite of what I imagined a nine-ties dot-com whiz kid would be, though he wasn't a start-up wunderkind, just a highly paid nine-to-fiver. He'd made his name building payroll systems. Pretty dull stuff, but I spent my days measuring concrete densities, so it's not like I could talk. He seemed willing to, though. I'd tracked him down after getting my hands on a list of Jim Connor's battalion and tracking them through the public service's various freedom of information sites. It's not easy to find out about government workers, but it's always possible. It's all public information, so if you're willing to dig, you can find a lot.

David Preston wasn't the only name I had, but he was the only one who now lived in Victoria, so I started with him. For about the millionth time, I thanked the Elders of the Internet for the invention of email. I did not want to cold call this guy. I found his email address at work using a very helpful Who Are We? page on the company's website. Pawz N Clawz could stand to talk to their webmaster.

To: david.preston@nsjsystems.ca

From: bguillemot@gmail.com

Subject: Cyprus 1980—1981

Dear Mr. Preston,

I believe that you may be the David
Preston who served in the Canadian
Peacekeeping mission in Cyprus during
1980 and 1981. I am looking for information about one of your colleagues, James
Masterson Connor. I believe that he may
be my father.

I am aware that Mr. Connor is deceased
and I was hoping you might be willing
to meet with me and share some of your
recollections of him. I can be reached by
phone or email.

I'd appreciate it if you got back to me,
and thank you for your time.

Sincerely,
Brian Guillemot

I have to give the ex-military man his due — he was prompt.

To: bguillemot@gmail.com

From: david.preston@nsjsystems.ca

Subject: Re: Cyprus 1980—1981

Mr. Guillemot

I would be happy to talk about Jim
Connor, I remember him well and it was
a sad day when he passed on. However, I
feel duty bound to inform you that I do
not believe that Jim had any children.
Regardless, if you would still like to
meet, please call my cell after 5 pm.

Cheers,
Dave Preston

WE MET AT THE STICKY WICKET. The bar is a Victoria landmark and, as such, its wares are generally overpriced and its atmosphere is generally underwhelming. That being said, everyone knows where it is and it's a safe place to meet just about anyone. I recognized him from the photo from his service record, even though nearly thirty years had passed. He'd kept in shape and looked like he could kill me with his bare hands if I looked at him funny.

I stepped over to the table where he sat nursing a pale beer and introduced myself. He stood and shook my hand more firmly than was necessary, then sat down again.

"So, you think Jimmy Connor was your dad?" he began without preamble.

I briefly explained what I knew and what I thought I knew, and David "Call me Dave" Preston listened silently. Eventually he shrugged.

"Could be, I guess," he said. "Jimmy never knew anything about it, I can tell you that for sure. My wife had our first just before I shipped out and old Jimmy was totally floored that I had a kid already. I was only twenty; things probably weren't all that different for me and Lorena than Jim and — what was her name again?"

"Kim."

"Yeah, those two. Anyway, I was a basket case with the new baby and not being there and everything. I think that was probably what put an end to my army career. I was sure I was going to be a lifer. But being away from Aaron and Lorena, well, it turned out I could handle everything else about the military life a hell of a lot better than that."

I nodded, wondering if he was going to talk about himself the whole time. "So, Jim talked about Kim a lot?" I prompted.

"Oh, sure," Dave said. "All he ever talked about was girls. He had about a half dozen of them on a string back home. All his down time he was either writing them letters or reading their letters to him. He was quite a ladies' man, your dad." He took a long drink of his beer and I tried to digest this information.

"Did he mention Kim?"

"Could be," Dave said. "I don't remember all the names. There was a Susan, Suzanne, something like that. And, of course, Barbara Ann. I couldn't forget her. Every time he mentioned her we'd all sing the song, you know, that old Beach Boys song." He thought for a moment; then a somewhat evil smile appeared on his lips. "Come to think of it, you might not be the only one. He did seem to get around, did old Jimmy."

"You saw this yourself?" I asked.

"Not a lot of women on the bases back then, son," Dave said, smirking. "But Jim was a good-looking fella, and the girls in town gave him the eye plenty. Sure, a lot of what he said sounded like so much talk, but if even half of it was true, little Kim wasn't the only mare in the stable."

"I see," I said.

"Look, buddy," Dave said. "This probably isn't what you wanted to hear about the fella you think is your old man. But you got to remember, he was just a kid. We all were. He was, what eighteen, nineteen years old? He was away from home for the first time, fighting in a war that had nothing to do with him, and most of what was going on was boring shit work that you would have got minimum wage for back home. So all there was to do was brag about all the girls you scored with. He wasn't a bad guy, Brian. He was just a guy. A young guy."

Dave shrugged again and drank some more of his beer. "There isn't much more to say. I only knew the guy for four months. You should try asking Kim — she probably knew him better than any of us ever did."

"Thanks," I said, trying to keep the bitterness from my voice.

"No problem, buddy," Dave said. "Glad to help."

SEEDY CAME OVER ON FRIDAY NIGHT with a bag full of Chinese food and a toothbrush. I picked at my Szechuan noodles and listened to her talk about some misfiling reference crisis at the library. After a while, she stopped. "What's wrong, Gumbo?" she said. "You usually snarf this stuff so fast I barely get a taste."

"I met up with one of Jim Connor's old army buddies this week," I said.

"And?"

"And it turns out that he was a grade-A asshole," I said.

"The buddy?" she asked.

"No," I said. "Connor."

"Oh."

"He was cheating on Kim," I said.

"Hm," Seedy said. "You think he knew she was pregnant?"

"The buddy seems pretty sure he didn't," I said.

"So, can you even be sure that he thought they were a couple?"

"What about the letters?" I said. "Why would he write to her all the time if they weren't?"

She shrugged. "Maybe," she said. "Maybe he was a dick, but don't forget, Gumbo — he was just a horny eighteen-year-old. Like you didn't do anything dumb when you were a teenager?"

My face reddened. The Thing with Jacquie. "It's not like I was stringing along a whole army of women while I was off on a goddamn peacekeeping mission," I said, masking my embarrassment with vehemence. "Making them think he was some kind of hero or something. Christ."

Seedy moved over to sit beside me and put her arm over my shoulder. "So he's no saint," she said. "What did you expect? You already knew he got a sixteen-year-old girl knocked up. That there were other girls shouldn't be all that shocking."

"I know," I said. "I just hoped that there would be something to hold on to, you know, something that I could look up to and respect. I wanted to come from somewhere good, somewhere noble." I was crying now and tried to move away from Seedy so she wouldn't see. It didn't work.

"You do come from somewhere great," she said. "Your mom and dad are genuine heroes, a crime fighter and a healer. What more noble background could you want?"

I sniffed and nodded and let her wipe the tears off my cheek. I let her lead me to the bed and then I let her help me forget David Preston and Jim Connor and Cyprus and the letters. I let her help me forget everything except that moment on the quad when she ate my chicken and cheese sandwich and I became the luckiest guy I knew.

31
HOME FOR CHRISTMAS

December 1, 1980
Dear Kimmie,

Thanks for the letters. They really make the days go by faster. I'm glad to hear that your brother is coming home for Christmas. It would suck to be stuck alone with your folks for the whole holiday.

Things here are fine. It's not so hot anymore, which is great, but when it rains everything turns to mud, which is a big pain in the butt. I'm getting tired of mop detail.

If you get a chance to go by my place, say hi to Roscoe for me. I miss the crabby old guy. April is only a few months away!

Jim

I AVOIDED KIM AND THE REST OF THE CLAN for months after that beer with Dave Preston. I didn't really think she'd ask me what I'd learned, but I couldn't be sure. And I wasn't sure that I'd be able not to say anything, either. I knew that it was really none of my business. The whole thing was just embarrassing, and I kind of wished I'd never looked into any of it.

Seedy had permanently moved a toothbrush and several changes of clothes into my apartment, and it became apparent that we were definitely seeing each other again. One night, over Indian takeout, we were talking about one of the local environmental foundations when she abruptly changed the topic.

"You still go over to your mom and dad's on Sundays?" she asked with a mouthful of chicken vindaloo.

I nodded. "Most weeks, yeah."

"You going this weekend?"

"Probably."

"Good," she said, and although I waited for her to continue, she just reached for the box of lamb korma.

"Why?" I finally asked.

"'Cause it would be good to see them again," she said. "It's been too long."

I was mopping up the last of the sauce on my plate with a piece of naan when I got it. "You want to come with," I said, the sound of dawning realization in my voice.

"Well, yeah," she said. "Why else would I mention it?"

"Why else, indeed?" I said, under my breath.

"That's okay, isn't it?" she asked, putting her plate down and fixing me with that stare that always worried me. "I mean, you're not hiding me from them or anything?"

"Of course not," I said. "But I ... uh ... haven't mentioned you to them, either."

"Jesus, Brian," she said. "We've been going out for, like, four months, now."

"More like three months and two weeks," I said, and she

glared at me. "It just hasn't come up," I said, not liking the wheedling I heard in my voice. She stared at me some more.

"I didn't know what to say," I admitted finally. "If we'd met again in the line at Thrifty's or something, I probably would have said something by now. But it was Chuck and Terry's wedding. I feel weird talking to them about anything to do with Kim now. So, it just never came up." I looked down at my feet. "I'm sorry."

"It's okay," she said. "But I'm coming this weekend. You don't have to tell them how we hooked up again, but if they ask I'm not going to lie. I'm sure they'll be cool. They've always been cool."

"Yeah," I said, but I didn't believe it for a second.

I TOLD THEM ON THE PHONE I was bringing my girlfriend. Dad said, "How come we haven't heard anything about her until now?"

"You have," I said, but didn't bother to explain. "We'll come over around two on Sunday, okay?"

"Okay," he said. "She isn't a vegetarian, is she?"

"No, Dad."

"Good," he said. "I was going to make ribs."

When we arrived, Mom immediately knew she recognized Seedy, but couldn't quite place her. Dad was fussing in the kitchen, probably still pouting over my lack of kibitzing about my love life.

"Have we met?" Mom asked Seedy as she held the door open.

"A long time ago, Ms. Holmes," Seedy said, grinning.

"Mom, this is Celia-Dee," I said. "Remember, from university? Seedy?"

Recognition flashed across Mom's face and she smiled widely. "Celia-Dee. The punk rocker. How nice to see you again." She gave me a significant glance that held a handful of questions, which I ignored. "Well." Mom took Seedy by the shoulders and drew her into the house. "You'd better come back and say hello to Dom. He'll be so thrilled to see you again. And I'm sure I asked you to call me Shirley."

"Thanks. And I'm just Celia these days," Seedy said. "Except to Gumbo here. He still calls me Seedy."

"Well, you should break him of that habit," Mom said archly. I rolled my eyes and toted our bag of salad, cookies and wine.

"It's okay," Seedy said. "I'll always be Seedy for him, anyway." I felt my stomach lurch in embarrassment, but Mom just smiled and ignored the double entendre. I hoped.

DINNER WAS NOT AS PAINFUL as I'd feared. Dad was, as Mom had guessed, thrilled to see Seedy. You'd have thought that she was *his* old girlfriend, not mine. He fussed around her, doling out platefuls of food and refilling her glass. I'd be the one doing the driving on the way home, that much was clear. It was okay, though. It was nice to see them so happy. Sunday dinners hadn't been very lively the past few months.

Seedy was her usual charming but strange self. She and Mom argued about the role of the police in political protests; then she spent about an hour educating Dad about the differences between punk, metal, hardcore and industrial. He even seemed to be interested.

I just watched as the three of them interacted and marvelled at my luck. I knew it was only a matter of time until we had The Fight, but none of the signs had appeared yet. I was trying not to think about the end and just enjoying the time we were having together. There is something marvellous about being with someone you've known for almost half your life. You have these common experiences, a common language already built into your relationship. It's almost as if you've been together the whole time, but you've had all this time apart to make things interesting. It made me wish I'd had more women friends.

I'd zoned out of the conversation, thinking about the family tree I was constructing for myself. I'd already decided to slot Jim Connor in as my birth father and was thinking about how to find more about his relatives. My mind had wandered off well into the wilderness when something Mom said reached me from the distance. I was immediately drawn back into the present and started to pay attention again.

"So, Brian must have told you his big news," she said, and I snapped back to see Seedy's face take on a quizzical expression.

"Oh?" she said nonchalantly.

"Yes," Mom continued, a smile on her face. "He found his birth mother. A lovely woman named Kim Heinz. They've met a few times now, I believe." She turned to me, and I went cold.

"Yeah," Dad picked up the thread. "It turns out that Brian has a bunch of half-siblings. We got to meet the whole family this summer. One of them was getting married — it was quite the gathering. Very interesting."

I glanced at Seedy and she looked at me. There was no way out of it, so I just shrugged and looked away. Seedy turned to my parents and smiled.

"I did know about that," she said. "Actually, that's how Brian and I reconnected. At the wedding. I'm a friend of Terry's, Charlotte's wife."

"Oh," Dad said, inquisitively, but with a tiny side of hurt in his voice.

"I didn't think you'd be interested in the wedding," I said.

"That's fine," Mom said, a false smile on her face. "It's just great that the two of you managed to meet up again. It's a funny world sometimes."

"It sure is," Seedy said, looking at me. "Full of all kinds of funny things and funny people, right?"

"Right," Dad said. "Speaking of which, do you have family here on the Island? I can't remember."

"My parents are divorced," Seedy said. "My dad lives in Vancouver and my mom moved to the States with her new husband. Why do you ask?"

"Well," Dad said, eyeing Mom, who seemed to know where

he was going with this, "we were thinking that if you didn't have other plans, it would be nice if you spent Christmas with us, here. Just a couple of days, but it would be good to have another mouth to eat all the food." He smiled hopefully at Seedy and then at me.

Seedy caught my eye and I smiled at her. "Sure," she said. "I'd love to. I wasn't planning on doing anything special and it would be nice to have a big winter feast. I haven't done that in a long time."

"No?" Dad asked.

"I don't see much of my mom anymore," Seedy explained. "She lives in Arizona, and it's too far and too expensive to travel very often. And I don't really get along with my dad ..." She broke off and Mom nodded at her.

"I understand," she said. "Not everyone has a close family."

"No," Seedy said, then turned to me. "You're all very lucky."

WE PACKED A WEEK'S WORTH OF CLOTHES into the Civic and drove out to my parents' place after work on December 23. Seedy had two whole weeks off for the holidays — the library just closed down for the duration. It was great because if you timed it right you'd get an extra two weeks on your loans. I'd taken out five DVDs. I booked only three days off the week after Christmas, but with the stat holidays I got ten days off. Maximizing annual leave was just one of the other useful skills I learned as part of the Competition Club.

It was dark by the time we arrived, but Mom had built a fire in the living room fireplace and had the kettle on. Within ten minutes our bags were stowed in the guest room — my room — and we had mugs of hot apple cider in our hands. It was like something out of a poorly written Hallmark movie of the week.

Seedy seemed happy enough and Dad liked having someone to fuss over. Mom seemed relaxed, and once she'd handed out the ciders she just curled up in her chair and threw a red tartan fleece blanket over her lap. "Isn't this nice?" she said when Dad had taken Seedy into the kitchen to show off the goodies he'd stocked in the fridge. "I'm so happy you and Celia reconnected, Brian. I always liked her, even though she put so much effort into trying to shock people. I always felt it was a bit of a shame that you two met so young."

"What do you mean?"

"Well," she said, sipping her cider, "hardly anyone finds the right person when they're a teenager. It takes a little living, a little bit of trying things out before you know what you really want in a partner. And you and Celia made such a good match that it seemed a shame to waste it on a youthful relationship."

"Huh," I said.

"It was such a pity when you two split up," she went on. "But now here you are. Together again." I suspected that she'd been spiking her cider.

"Don't get too attached," I said morosely. "Nothing lasts."

She frowned. "Is there something wrong?" she asked. "You two having trouble?"

"No, nothing like that," I said, wishing we could stop talking about this. "I just ... Things don't ever last, is all." I tried to put an air of finality into the conversation, and she must have understood because she didn't say anything else about it. But she didn't look convinced. Not one bit.

32
FIRST THE POTATOES

December 18, 1980

Dear Kimmie,

I got a letter from Mom. She says you're going by the house once a week to see Roscoe and the other birds. You don't know how much this means to me. He really likes you, you know. I don't know anyone who's as good with him as you are. Mom thinks he's a menace. It makes me feel better being here knowing that you're still taking care of him.

It's getting festive around here, though it's strange not to have any rain or cold at Christmas. The guys from the interior are going crazy, they're used to snow. It's just not Christmas without snow, they say. You

should come out to the Island, I tell them.
We're still counting the flowers in December.

There probably aren't really any flowers
blooming now, I guess. But I always imagine you
with a bundle of daisies, like you used to pick
in the summer behind the house. I guess it
doesn't hurt to imagine summer here, where it
never even gets cold.

Say hi to Roscoe for me and if you see my
mom thank her for the letter.

Jim

ON CHRISTMAS EVE we didn't do much. Dad got us going on a
cards tournament, in which Seedy tried to teach us how to play
contract bridge. We kind of got the hang of bidding, but we all
did much better at hearts and cribbage. The day disappeared in
a haze of cards, cookies, wine and Dad's home-smoked salmon.
I didn't know he'd started doing that and it turned out he was
great at it. We ate our faces off.

Seedy turned in at about ten with a large book she'd brought
along. I stayed up, strangely enjoying the warm company of
my mom and dad. We were just chatting aimlessly the way
people do. Mom had asked about my current project at work,
and I could tell I was droning on. They seemed not to mind, so
I didn't bother to stop myself.

More wine was consumed and soon spiked apple ciders appeared from the kitchen. "How's Kim?" Mom asked out of the blue.

"Uh, fine, I guess," I said. I could almost feel Dad staring at me. "I, uh, haven't talked to her in a while."

"You did send her a Christmas card, didn't you?" That was Mom. Who never sent anyone a Christmas card in her life.

"Uh ..."

"Really, Brian," Dad said, "after she was kind enough to invite you — to invite us *all* into her family, the least you could do is put yourself out a little and keep in touch."

"I will," I said. "I am. It's just been ... busy, you know? Work, Seedy. I'll send Kim an email, promise." Dad seemed appeased, but Mom had that look. The one that I always imagined she used on suspects that says *I don't believe a word of it, scuzzball.* Luckily, Dad got sidetracked by my mention of Seedy.

"Is Celia okay? She's been gone a while."

"She went up to bed," I said. "It's been busy at her work all week. It's the price of being closed down for two weeks — lots of work before the holiday. I think she's just tired. Plus, she's had her nose in that book ever since she picked it up. She's been bringing it with her everywhere she goes, even over to my place." I waited for the blush to appear on my face at the obvious insinuation of what Seedy would be doing at my apartment, but it didn't seem to come. Embarrassment frightened off by excessive wine consumption, I guess. It never worked that way before, but it might just be one of the perks of age.

"Seems pretty serious between you two," Dad said. Mom shot him a look, and I scowled at them both.

"Jeez, you guys," I said. "You both seem to have us married off already. We've only been going out for a couple of months."

"Sure," Mom said, "but it's not like with other girls. You know her, you already know each other. It's not really just a couple of months at all. All the time you've known each other counts, Brian. It counts."

"Shirley," Dad said, smiling at Mom, "don't push them. They're still just kids, you know that."

"We were married and already fighting with the agency by the time we were their age," she shot back.

"It was different then," Dad said weakly. I sighed. Then I paid attention to what Mom had said.

"What do you mean, 'fighting with the agency'?"

"Oh, it's not that interesting," Mom said airily. "Obviously, it all worked out in the end."

"Dad." I hoped he was less drunk or at least more forthcoming. "What is she talking about?"

"Well," he said, sipping his cider, "it took a long time and a lot of paperwork to finally bring you home for good. We were busy with government and non-government agencies for a good couple of years. It was really frustrating, especially since we'd been your foster parents from almost the day you were born. There was just a lot of bureaucracy."

"But my birth certificate," I said. "It shows you as my parents from when I was born."

"They backdate them," Mom said. "It's a legal thing, even when kids are adopted at an older age. We had a hard time making it official, though. For a while there it looked like we might lose you. It was a tough time, right, Dom?"

"I haven't thought about it for years," Dad said, his voice far away. "It was horrible."

"What was the problem?" I asked.

"The problem was there was no problem," Dad said. I frowned and he explained. "Most couples choose adoption because they can't get pregnant on their own. The agency we went through expected a medical report confirming the infertility of the couple when you apply for adoption."

"I still don't think that was legal," Mom said.

Dad shrugged. "What did we know?" he said.

"I don't get it," I said. "What was the problem?"

"Well, we didn't have the report," Dad said. "And it made life difficult."

"Why didn't you have the report?" I asked.

"Because we're not infertile," Mom said. "At least, we don't think so. It's pretty unlikely."

"I'm confused," I said. "If you could have kids, why ..."

"There are too many people on this planet, Brian," Dad said. "We both believed that then and we believe it even more so now. But we wanted to be parents. So, the obvious choice was to adopt a baby who was already born. But the bureaucracy didn't understand that as a reason, so we had to jump through hoops to finally get to be your parents. It was awful." He looked at Mom, then added, "But as your mom said, everything worked out in the end. And we couldn't be happier." He beamed at me, a happily drunken smile that I felt reflected in my own face.

"I love you guys," I said.

"We love you too, honey," Mom said.

I WENT TO BED AND FOUND SEEDY FAST ASLEEP, her mouth hanging open and her book face down on her chest. I carefully picked up the book, marked her place and put it on the nightstand. I tried to slip into bed quietly, but I woke her up anyway.

"What time is is?" she asked groggily.

"About one in the morning," I whispered. "Go back to sleep."

"We're going to miss Santa," she said and rolled over, her arm over my chest. She fell asleep again and I listened to the sound of her breathing into my neck. All of a sudden, I was consumed with sadness at the thought there would inevitably come a day when this wouldn't happen anymore.

A tiny drunken voice in my mind screamed at me to quit worrying and just enjoy the moment, but then I fell asleep and it was gone.

WE'D NEVER BEEN BIG GIFT GIVERS in the Holmes–Guillemot house, and the first time around Seedy and I hadn't had any money, so presents just never came up. But this time there were a few wrapped parcels under the avocado plant from whose branches Dad had strung some bits of tinsel and hung an odd assortment of decorations. I wondered where they'd come from. I couldn't see either Mom or Dad actually spending money on something like that. I stashed the few gifts I'd brought in a clear space near the plant pot and inspected the ornaments.

They were entirely mismatched: a Snoopy on his doghouse wearing a Santa hat, a plastic snowflake with *1993* written on it in red-and-green glitter, an expensive-looking cut-glass dove, an incongruous menorah on a string. I was fingering a scary-looking plastic Santa when Mom came in. "I don't really understand why people give us Christmas tree ornaments," she said, a cup of coffee in her hand. "I mean, if you don't know someone well enough to know whether or not they decorate for Christmas, do you really need to give them a gift?"

"These were all presents?"

"Yup," she said. "Mostly from co-workers of mine or your dad's."

I looked at the motley collection. "What's with the menorah?" I asked.

"Oh, that," Mom laughed. "That was Bill Driscoll trying to be sensitive."

Driscoll was one of the other long-serving cops on the Saanich Police Force. Mom must have worked with him for a dozen years. "What do you mean?" I asked.

"We were talking about the holidays in the squad room one day and it came up that I wasn't a Christian. Bill is one of those weird Christmas fans, you know, wears reindeer ties all through December, decorates his cubicle, that sort of thing. Anyway, he got my name in the Secret Santa pool and I guess he couldn't figure out what to do for a non-Christian. So, voilà."

"Does he think we're Jewish?"

"Naw," she said. "He's just an idiot."

I laughed. Mom had never badmouthed any of her co-workers before. "What's all the hilarity?" Dad asked as he walked into the room. "You're not making fun of my beautiful Yule Arbour, are you?"

"Not in the least," Mom said, kissing him on the cheek. "I think it's lovely."

"What's that?" Seedy said, finally unable to sleep any more through the racket we all were making, I guess. "The smell of coffee? I'd say it's pretty lovely."

"Let me get you a cup, dear," Dad said, slipping into the kitchen. "And how does lox and bagels sound for breakfast?"

"Fantastic," Seedy said. "I need to come over here more often."

Dad smiled happily and Mom turned to Seedy. "I think that would be wonderful, Celia," she said.

"It's not always lox and bagels," I said, trying for lightheartededness. "It's just as likely to be cereal and frozen orange juice."

"Well, I like those, too," Seedy said, rescuing the conversation by beaming at Mom. "So, what's the program here? My mom and I used to open presents in the morning, then spend the rest of the day cooking, eating and playing games. How does it work around here?"

"Pretty much the same," Mom said. "Dom does most of the cooking — I'm sure he'd accept assistance if you were so inclined, but don't feel obliged. It's a pretty casual affair; usually we just roast a chicken or something. Since you're here, Dom got fancy and we have a goose. I hope you like dark meat."

"Sounds great," Seedy said. "Uh, Dom isn't going to be stuck in the kitchen all day, is he?"

"No," Dad said, coming back with a large mug of coffee for Seedy and a platter of bagels, cream cheese and thin smoked salmon slices. "Once I get everything going, it won't take long. And I couldn't help but overhear, so if you feel like peeling a few potatoes I wouldn't object. Otherwise, I've got it all in hand." He grinned and sat down, passing out small plates for the food. We loaded up and ate.

It didn't take long to open the gifts. I got Mom one of the fancy desk calendars she liked but wouldn't buy herself because they were too expensive. I got Dad a DVD set of the most recent season of a weird Japanese game show he loved, which I'd had to special order months before. He was visibly excited when he ripped off the paper. Mom rolled her eyes — she didn't see the show's appeal — and passed me a large box.

It was very light and I couldn't stop myself from shaking it. Mom and Dad smirked at each other and I saw Seedy stifling a grin. "Are you in on this?" I asked her.

"I say nothing," she said, affecting a silly accent. I scowled, but felt a strange warmness inside when I realized that she must have talked to my parents about whatever this was. I carefully removed the ribbon and tape holding the paper to the box, folding it and setting it aside. I slit the tape holding the lid of the box closed and opened it, finding nothing but bubble wrap. I arched an eyebrow and popped a bubble between my thumb and forefinger.

"I do like popping bubble wrap," I said. "Thanks, guys."

"Keep looking," Dad said, taking a bite of bagel. I took out all the plastic and at the bottom of the box saw an envelope. It was a plain number-ten envelope with what felt like a couple of folded sheets inside. Seedy grinned, and Mom and Dad were smiling widely now, too. I felt conspicuous and strange. I opened the envelope and found a gift certificate for a week at a luxury surf camp in Tofino.

"This is ..." I didn't know what to say. "How did you know?" I asked them all.

"You mentioned it once," Seedy said. "Back in university. I remembered."

"Wow," I said. "And you told them and ..."

"It just came up in conversation," she said. "Then your mom called and asked if I thought it would be a good gift and I said yeah. I hope you like it."

"Totally gnarly," I said, feeling foolish. I handed Seedy her gift, a silver necklace I'd noticed her eyeing in one of the little boutiques in Fan Tan Alley. She put it on and I saw her eyes glow. Mom and Dad exchanged a glance and I sighed, hopefully quietly.

Then Seedy pulled out a box not too dissimilar to the one my parents had given me. "What's this?" I asked.

"It's from me," she said. I opened it carefully as always and found inside a heavy, rattly box labelled *Power Grid*. I turned it over and looked at Seedy, puzzled.

"It's a game," she said. "I played it before; I think you'll like it. Trust me." I'd never been a big fan of board games;

Monopoly made me want to scream. I could barely stand Scrabble with Mom and Dad.

"Thanks," I said, weakly. I looked at the copy on the bottom and thought the game sounded pretty different from anything else I'd ever played. "Three to six players," I read. "Hrm."

"I thought we could invite your friends over sometime," Seedy said. "Johnny and maybe Blair and Angela, too."

"Huh," I said, sensing an entire strategy in the guise of this gift. "Well, why don't we open it up and give it a try?"

"First," Dad said, "we peel the potatoes."

33
THE PAJAMA GAME

December 25, 1980
Dear Kimmie,

Merry Christmas! I have to admit it's
not that merry around here. I don't want to
get all sappy in my letters, it doesn't help
anything. But I really miss you. The guys all
got each other little presents like a pack of
smokes or a bottle of ouzo, but none of that
is helping. All I want is to be home with you.

I hope you are having a good holiday. Try
and stop in to see Mom and the others, I know
they'd love to see you.

I don't have much to say this time, it's
just kind of tough here right now. But it's
not for too much longer, then I'll be home.

I miss you.

Jim

SEEDY GAVE ME TWO WEEKS' GRACE before she started threatening to cold call Johnny, Blair and Angela. She'd never even
met Blair and Ange and she was ready to invite them over for a
games night. I was horrified.

So, of course her ploy worked and I invited them myself.

The first time they came over was a Friday night, and I'd
had a hell of a week at work. I was tired and cranky and the last
thing I wanted was to have a houseful of people over. But the
three of them and Seedy had all planned to come, so it was on
and I couldn't do anything about it. I'd bought a case of beer, a
couple of bottles of bubbly water for Angela and twenty bucks'
worth of snacks. When I got home, I got the Romeo's delivery
pizza menu out and the phone ready to go.

Seedy arrived first and dumped her now very familiar over-
night bag in my bedroom. She looked great and smelled fantastic. I wished that the others weren't coming, but now for an
entirely different reason. I told her so and she grabbed my butt
and whispered, "I'll make waiting worth your while." I was
lucky that Johnny didn't turn up for another ten minutes.

When he did arrive, he kissed Seedy on the cheek and gave
me a leer. It turned out that they'd known each other in university and spent five minutes lying to each other about how neither
of them had changed. I busied myself in the kitchen arranging
Johnny's contribution of expensive pastries on a plate. I'd just
gotten them out to the table when the buzzer sounded again.

Angela was huge, but it didn't seem to bother her. "I'm just
so happy that the puking is over," she said. "I don't care how
big I am so long as that's done with." She loaded up a plate

with about half of Johnny's quiches and pies, and poured a large glass of water. "Don't mean to be rude," she said. "Eating for two here."

"Two elephants, maybe," Blair said, but he grinned and Angela smiled back. "So you're the famous Seedy P." He turned to Seedy.

"It's just Celia these days," she said, jerking her head in my direction. "He's the only one who hasn't moved with the times in the nomenclature department."

"Old dogs, eh?" Angela said, swallowing a mouthful of something.

"It's okay," she said. "Makes me feel like a young punk again."

"Guys," I said, "I'm right here. You don't have to talk about me as if I were off in Siberia or something."

"Sorry, Gumbo," Angela said. "So, where's the rest of the food?"

We ordered a couple of pizzas, one with a half of pineapple and jalapeño for Angela, then cracked open the game.

Seedy had been on the money: I did like the game. I had no idea there were board games like this and was starting to look forward to a night of playing. We explained the rules to the others and were partway through the opening phase when the pizzas arrived. We ate over the board, stopping to open beers and get more snacks.

When we got to the third round, all of us except Angela were pretty drunk. "So, are you guys going to move in together?" Johnny asked Seedy as he rolled the dice. "As they say in *The Pajama Game*, 'Two can sleep as cheap as one.'"

"*The Pajama Game?*" I asked incredulously.

"It's a musical," he said, as if that explained everything. "So, are you?"

"Maybe," Seedy said, shooting me a sideways glance. We had not talked about this possibility before. "It's still kind of soon for that."

"How long did you guys go out before you shacked up?" Johnny asked Blair and Angela.

"A year, maybe two?" Angela said, looking to Blair for confirmation.

"About nineteen months, if you want to be exact," he said, grinning. "But there was a chunk of time when Ange was travelling for work, so that doesn't really count."

"I don't think there's a particular amount of time you need to date before you know," Angela said. "When you know, you know." She gave Seedy and me a pointed look, then said, "I'm buying two units of uranium. Fork it over, Johnny."

WE DIDN'T TALK ABOUT IT FOR A WHILE, but some time before Valentine's Day, Seedy said, "So if we lived together, would we buy a place, do you think?"

"Jeez, Seedy," I said, pausing the DVD we were watching. "Do you really want to take that step? I mean, things are great now. Don't fix it if it ain't broke."

"I'm not saying we have to do it now," she said. "But I'm over here all the time. It's kind of dumb not to talk about it, at least."

"Damn it, Seedy," I said, then looked away. I had finally managed to put the inevitability of The Fight out of my mind and just be happy. Now this talk of moving in together had smashed the wall that had been keeping those thoughts at bay. I was filled with a sense of dread and sadness, as if we'd already broken up.

"What's wrong, BeeGee?" she said, real concern in her voice. "You're not one of those commitment-phobic guys. Hell, that's more my line. What's eating you?"

"Damn it, Seedy," I repeated, trying to keep my voice even. "It never works out. And it's just going to be so much worse if we're living together when it does ..."

"What are you talking about?" she said, her voice authoritative and compelling.

"It's the birth control thing," I blurted. "Every girlfriend I've ever had, after you, left me because of the birth control thing. And it will happen with us, too; it always does. So, let's just forget it, okay? I don't want to talk about it."

"The birth control thing?" she said incredulously. "What the fuck are you talking about?"

I wished the earth would open up and swallow me whole, but I stared at my feet and explained as best I could about condoms and infidelity and Audrey and Beth and the rest of it. I have to give her credit: Seedy didn't laugh. She didn't even smirk. She did, however, take my hand in hers and grab my face. She looked me deeply and intensely in the eye. I didn't know how to look away and somehow didn't want to.

"I guess I can see how some women might feel that way," she said, "but I don't."

"I know, but ..."

"Don't 'but' me," she said. "I know myself well enough to know something like this. I don't want children, Brian, you know that. And I know you don't want children — it's one of the many, many things that makes us so good together. I also don't really want to take hormonal birth control, so using condoms works just fine for me. I don't see that changing if we live together. Besides," she said, her lips finally tugging up into a grin, "I like men and all, but I can't get past the fact that jizz is really gross."

That broke the spell and I started to laugh. "What?" she said, punching me in the arm and faking a pout. "Well, it is."

"I love you, Celia-Dee," I said when I'd finally finished laughing.

"I know you do, Brian Gumbo," she said and snuggled into my arms while hitting play on the remote control.

JOHNNY AND BLAIR AND ANGELA came to our housewarming, along with three-week-old Marty. Seedy had invited some of her co-workers, including Terry, who, of course, brought Chuck. I hadn't seen either of them since the wedding and it was obvious that married life suited them.

"I was talking to Mom the other day," Chuck said when she caught up with me in the giant eat-in kitchen of the condo

Seedy and I had bought. "She said she hasn't heard from you in a while. Everything okay?"

"Yeah," I said. "I found out some stuff about my father and I know Kim's a little ... sensitive about it. I just didn't know what to say."

"Huh," Chuck said. "Well, you don't have to say anything about it if you don't want. I don't think that's what's on her mind. I think she'd just like to hear from you, but now that the wedding's over she doesn't have an excuse to get in touch. She's like that."

"Yeah," I said. "I know the feeling."

Terry walked in with Angela then and said, "There you two are. I was just talking with Angela here about volunteering to feed the homeless for a couple of days a month. What a great opportunity, right?"

She grinned at us, grabbed a couple of drinks for the two of them and they walked back out to the party. Chuck said, "Well, at least it's the homeless that's got Terry all fired up."

"What do you mean?" I asked.

"I was afraid it was the baby," Chuck said. "We've only been married a few months; I'm not ready for that yet."

"I hear ya, sister," I said as we clinked beer cans.

34
ALWAYS AND FOREVER

I **SENT KIM AN EMAIL** the week after the housewarming. I didn't actually have anything to say, but I managed to pick a few random small-talk phrases out of the air and I guess it did the trick. It took a few days before she replied, long enough that I wondered if I'd somehow screwed it all up and she was done talking to me. But soon enough the reply came, chatty and ill-punctuated as always.

```
hi brian

good to hear from you. im going to be
in town in a few weeks and it will be
your birthday soon! we should have lunch
or something. i liked that place we met
before, why dont we go there?

ill let you know for sure when ill be
in town but keep the first few weeks of
april free!
kim
```

For some reason, it struck me as odd that Kim would know when my birthday was. Obviously, once I thought about it, it was entirely reasonable that she'd remember the date. But it had become evident to me that I thought of Kim and the others

— Chuck, Rob and Jeannette — as people who belonged to my adult life. I didn't know them when I was a kid, so it felt strange to have Kim refer to something that I know I'd never mentioned to her.

Regardless, I opened the calendar on my phone and booked off lunchtimes for the first three weeks of April and the last week of March. I didn't make many lunch dates, but just in case, I didn't want to have to cancel on anyone. I wanted to leave any date available for Kim. I felt like I'd been somehow delinquent after all the time we'd spent together in the summer that we hadn't seen each other in over six months. Who'd have guessed that double the mothers means double the guilt?

WE MET AT ELEVEN THIRTY and I'd booked off the afternoon. I didn't know how long she would have, but it seemed like I ought to give her some time. It felt strange to be meeting her without the rest of them. What if we had nothing to talk about? I was nearly as nervous as the last time I'd been at this table by the window, watching for a woman I wouldn't recognize but who was my mother. I ordered too many cups of coffee from Françoise and fidgeted with my phone.

Kim arrived a couple of minutes late and breezed over to the table. I stood and she kissed me lightly on the cheek as if I were a socialite acquaintance. "Good to see you, Brian," she said. "You're looking well."

"Thanks," I said, sitting. "You, too." And she was looking well, indeed. It was like now that the wedding stress was gone, five years of aging went with it. I was amazed at how youthful and energetic she was.

"I guess it's good genes," she said and laughed. I smiled. We ordered lunch and soon settled into a chatty routine. "So, what's new and exciting?" she asked.

"A lot, I guess," I said, frowning as I thought about it. "Remember that woman I was with at Charlotte's wedding?"

"Sure," she said, grinning. "The 'coincidence'." She made air quotes with her fingers when she said the last word.

"Yeah," I said. "Well, we bought a condo last month."

"Good for you," Kim said, genuine excitement in her voice. "You did seem like she was something special last summer. What's her name?"

"Oh, jeez," I said, "I'm sorry. It's Celia. Her name is Celia-Dee Pavane. I call her Seedy; it's kind of a long story ... anyway."

"You said you knew her from before," she quizzed me as our sandwiches arrived. "From where?"

"She was my first real girlfriend," I said. "We went out for about six months in university."

Kim stopped chewing and put her sandwich down. "Young love," she said, but the phrase didn't have an iota of the patronizing tone most people endow it with. "It's none of my business," she said, "but why did it end, back then?"

"I don't really know," I said. "At the time there was a reason, but it never made sense, not then, not now." I put down my own sandwich and wiped my fingers on my napkin as I thought. "I think it was just that we were too young and we knew it. We were pretty great together, but we were just kids. We weren't ready to meet The One, you know? So we just pushed each other away, because we were scared that otherwise we'd be stuck together forever." I caught her eye and was intimidated by the intensity of her gaze. "Well, that's sort of how it seems now," I backpedalled. "You know, now that we're together again."

"It's hard when you meet the love of your life when you're young," she said with a certain air of knowledge. "You're both very lucky that you managed to meet again. That's uncommon for people like you two."

"I know," I said. "It sometimes feels like we've just missed a catastrophe, like we've been given a second chance. Sounds crazy, huh?"

"No," she said, and I got the impression she was trying to hold back tears. "Not crazy at all." She cleared her throat and looked out the window for a long time. I picked up my sandwich and took a bite. Then she said, not turning her gaze from the street outside, "When you're young and you've actually found true love, when you've found the person who you should spend your life with, and then it's over ..." She blinked a few times and took a breath.

"Nothing else ever lives up to that," she said finally. "You've got this memory of the way things ought to be and, no matter what happens, no matter who you meet and what life brings, it just can't compare to that memory. It's sort of like a part of you stops back then. Like some fundamental aspect of you never gets any older than you were back when all roads led to a future where you were happy, where you were loved."

She continued staring out the window, and as I followed her gaze I noticed that she didn't seem to be seeing anything that was going on in the street. A man walked past with a clown wig on and her eyes didn't even flutter in his direction. She was a million miles away — or maybe only thirty years away.

There wasn't much to say to that, so I left her alone with her thoughts as I finished my sandwich. She came back to reality a few minutes later and, as if nothing had ever happened, said, "So, I don't know if you've heard or not but Rob and Anna are finally getting married."

"Not another wedding," I said, grinning.

"No worries," Kim replied. "They're going to elope to Fiji. After Chuck and Terry, they decided to just skip all the hoopla."

"Good for them," I said, thinking about the madness avoidance, but I think Kim took my remark as an endorsement of their pending nuptials. No need to correct her on that, I figured.

We gossiped about the rest of the kids and I told her a little about Blair and Angela and their new baby. Before long, Françoise came out to let us know that she was going to close in a half hour and I looked at my phone in astonishment. It was after three o'clock in the afternoon. Kim grinned at me. "That's what happens when you try to pack half a year into one lunch. Takes time."

"I'll try to be better," I said, sheepishly.

"Don't worry about it," Kim said. "You don't owe me anything and I know that life gets in the way. All the time. Just don't forget that I really am happy that you found me after all these years and it would be a shame to just let all this slip away."

I nodded. We walked out of Café Mozart together, after

leaving a generous tip for Françoise, and I walked with Kim to where her car was parked.

"This was really nice," I said. "Maybe next time you could come over to our place. Seedy makes a great veggie lasagna."

"That sounds great," Kim said, touching my arm lightly. "Oh, before I forget, I have something for you. Call it a birthday present." I frowned in surprise, as she opened the rear door of her car and took a large envelope out of the back seat. "I'll want these back," she said, "but I think it's time you got to look at them." She reached up and pecked me on the cheek again, then was in the car, belted and off down the road before I had a chance to ask what it was.

WHEN I GOT HOME, Seedy was already there. It had been her day off and she'd been out shopping. She'd filled the fridge and there was a set of takeout boxes on the counter waiting for me.

"So, how did it go?" she asked.

"Good," I said and briefly filled her in on the conversation.

"Wow," she said. "Fiji, eh? That's a hell of a long flight just to avoid a huge family event."

"What?" I said, still focussed on the envelope. It was a boring-looking manila envelope, with what I guessed were about ten or so folded sheets inside. It smelled old, not musty, but like the pages had been handled over and over again over many years. I still hadn't opened it.

Seedy laughed at me. "Okay, go ahead already. Open your present. I'll leave you alone until you're done." She kissed me, running her hand lightly over my hair in a gesture that I'd come to feel was as much a sense of home as a place to put my keys and find my toothbrush. I watched her walk into the second bedroom we used as a joint study, and she looked back at me.

"When you get back from your trip through history," she said, "I'll be here."

THERE WERE EIGHT LETTERS, each one was no more than two pages long and written on old-fashioned, tissue-thin blue air-mail paper. The writing was neat and orderly, but I got a sense from the workmanlike cursive that they were somehow challenging to write.

When I saw the date on the first, I knew what they were. I inhaled the scent of my father's ink and felt a prickling behind my eyes.

October 22, 1980
Dear kimmie,

I thought it would be hot here, but it's not that bad.

I READ THEM THROUGH IN ONE SHOT, one after the other like I was unable to stop. It probably took less than half an hour, but I felt like I was living an entire lifetime through those thousand words. When I finished the last letter, I wiped the wetness from my cheeks, got up and walked over to the other room to take the woman I loved in my arms and never let her go.

January 9, 1981
Happy New Year!

Thanks for the Christmas card and the chocolate bar. It got mooshed a little in the mail, but it still tastes great. I'm limiting myself to one square a day, I don't want it to end. Every time I taste it, I think of you.

You'll like this: Mom has been sending me letters that she pretends are written by the birds. It's pretty funny to get a letter from Suzie Q or Barbara Ann. The other guys all think they are my girlfriends. I don't mind. I don't really want to talk to them about you, it seems kind of gross, the way they are about girls. So I pretend I have five girlfriends and laugh when they ask about Rose (that's what I call Roscoe).

Mom says you still come by to play with the birds. She says she wishes you could take them home with you, but I know your folks won't let you. When I get back, I'll have enough money to get a place of our own while I'm at veterinary school and we can take all the birds. I even want to take Roscoe, that biting, scratching bad-ass. Mom says he's so much nicer when you're around.

    Less than four months until April. Then I can see all my ladies (ha ha), especially my number one lady.

    I miss you, Kim.

Love, always and forever,
Jim

ACKNOWLEDGEMENTS

THANKS FIRST AND FOREMOST to my editor, Leslie Vermeer. Her boundless enthusiasm for this project was a joy to behold, and her keen eye helped make this a much better book. The rest of the crew at NeWest have also been fantastic, especially Claire Kelly and Matt Bowes. It's delightful to work with such competent and passionate people.

I owe a great debt to Amanda Witherell, whose tales of growing up in a veritable menagerie were the seeds that grew into this book. Her knowledge of bird-things and excellent critical reading were invaluable. All errors are mine.

Thanks to Brian Twitchell for letting me borrow his name and for the many beers and laughs.

My many writing friends online and off keep the weasels at bay and have made me a better writer. Thank you all.

Finally, thanks to Steven Ensslen for everything. Always and forever.

DARUSHA writes science fiction and speculative poetry as M. Darusha Wehm and mainstream poetry and fiction as Darusha Wehm. Science fiction books include *Beautiful Red, Children of Arkadia* and the Andersson Dexter cyberpunk detective series. Mainstream books include the Devi Jones' Locker Young Adult series and *The Home for Wayward Parrots*.

Darusha's short fiction and poetry have appeared in many venues, including *Arsenika, Nature, Escape Pod* and several anthologies.

Darusha is originally from Canada but currently lives in Wellington, New Zealand, after spending the past several years sailing the Pacific. For more information, visit http://darusha.ca.